MW00791830

REVERSE PERFECTION

A Memoir

ABBY REDTREE

Printed in the United States of America.

ISBN   Hardback   978-1-64361-263-8
              eBook   978-1-64361-264-5

Westwood Books Publishing LLC
10389 Almayo Ave, Suite 103
Los Angeles, CA 90064

www.westwoodbookspublishing.com

1

Casey waited with Randy in the Ambassadors Lounge Saturday at Kennedy Airport for their flight to London to be called. They had tried to return to Europe at least yearly since they were married, and sometimes more often, if business required.

Randy's business was doing exceptionally well in spite of a bad economy and he was able to have Casey be one of David Alan's primary motivating factors in the business. She created a division of sportswear for the active, upwardly mobile person and was now getting the itch to do something that would be a tremendous challenge and gamble and a departure from the David Alan image. She was a creative and strong person.

This trip was to be particularly exciting because they had decided to take the Orient express to Istanbul after spending a few days in London with some friends that they had met in Acapulco. Biorj, who was Swedish, was responsible for Casey's designing and also modeled for her in New York, London and Paris.

Casey knew this was going to be a great trip because Biorj was fiendishly running around with her more excited than ever; her beautiful long straight blonde hair was glowing from the sunlight, and the radiance of her deep turquoise eyes was more prevalent than ever against her soft porcelain like skin which had the remnants of a summer tan from the South of France. Her features were perfect and her cheekbones high. She had the love of life in her face and body. She was so worried about her age, though. She was a vision as beautiful as she had looked when she discovered Randy and Casey nibbling fruit on their patio, she looking up from her lounge.

We all met, when she was resting on a lounge beneath our villa. Randy and Casey were nibbling apples, bananas, pears and kumquats on their patio at Las Brisa's in Acapulco which was in perfect view of Biorj, who lay listless below in a croceted bikini barely covering her most private of private parts. This was quite a turn on to the lover's

Sharing a pitcher of Margaritas, Randy motioned to Biorj to come and join them in a fit of friendly embarrassment.

Casey always traveled with the right clothes but Biorj was especially interested in sending her on the train with the right clothes and jewelry. Usually Casey didn't even bother with jewelry. Casey wasn't too preoccupied with how she looked because she knew she dressed well and looked great.

After a wonderful dinner at Waltan's with Biorj and her husband Michael, Randy and Casey kissed goodnight, never dreaming that either of them would be aroused, but something magical drew the two of them together to two and a half hours of gratification and satisfaction.

After brunch at Brown's, they rushed off to Victoria Station in Biorj's limousine to bid them farewell. It was a magnificent site. What opulence. Randy always managed to look so dashingly handsome with his boyish smile and muscular physique, which would put him at least ten years behind his contemporaries. Of course, long distance running added to the strength, and allowed him to eat like a glutton. He looked so trim in his dark suit and raincoat, his dark eyes had something sweetly provocative and sensitive about them, and his handsome but innocent, almost naive boyish manner was really what made Casey fall head over heels in love with him. Randy not only had a playful quality about him, but he could be serious and tough and controlling, at least he tried to be. He was a strong man. He was a man.

Casey knew this was an unusual combination and she knew that she must spend the rest of her life with Randy Edwards.

Casey's blonde hair was hanging straight off of her face and her greenish-brown eyes were fresh and gorgeous in spite of the fact that they had had very little sleep the night before. Her five foot six trim, well-proportioned body looked great in the St. Laurent pants suit that Biorj and she had picked. Casey and Randy always managed to complement each other, they looked so good together.

The moment preceding the departure of the train were filled with flowers, champagne, the best service, and the anticipation of what the next few days would uncover. The Orient Express was the adventure, part of their journey together.

Randy and Casey settled in their cabins. Randy was fortunate enough to know how claustrophobic the cabins are and ordered two adjoining which gave a little more room to spread out, especially Casey's wardrobe. It was the best one can do on the train and probably the only way to travel, especially in the summer when you can be sure that there is no air except fresh air.

Casey and Randy got settled and were anxious to explore. The train was beautifully appointed with Victorian lamps and beautiful needlepoint fabrics, the silver, glass and marble were all so authentic you really felt like they were original, even if some had been newly acquired for the refurbishing of the train. The people were elegant and well dressed and Casey remarked to Randy that everyone was friendly, social and quite cordial. One did not feel that he was being observed by the next person nor did you feel at all that you had to impress anyone. There was just sort of an understanding of equanimity. It really was so elegant and opulent, a feeling that Casey knew that she hadn't experienced since she was a child growing up at her parents mansion. It also occurred to her that it was a good feeling not the pressured, competitive feeling that she felt when she was with the girls in her crowd. However, Casey always dealt well with competition because she was always lucky enough to always be able to have what she wanted and she sometimes had the feeling that

Randy resented this, but they would talk about it and she knew that Randy was stronger than she and that he taught her a great deal of her strength and character. His background was so similar to hers and they were both very resistant to stress.

Randy was extremely confident and independent, not only about himself as a person, but monetarily too. He was too spoiled to be with anyone who wasn't totally in touch with themselves, and Casey and Randy found a rare combination in each other, along with having an intense physical attraction toward each other.

Now that they were unpacked, Randy was anxious and curious to see the Club Car and have dinner and browse. As they walked into the Club Car they were overwhelmed by the beautifully appointed mahogany bar which looked as if it were freshly polished. The porters, in immaculate white jackets and gloves and white tie, what a spectacle.

Casey remembered being seated in the middle of the car and entering very comfortably into the conversation circle. Randy was about to order drinks and as Casey told the porter that she wanted a Grey Goose on the rocks with a lemon twist, she felt a piercing glance from across the club car.

Randy had heard very little about Peter Munson. Peter had always known Daddy and been a friend of the family even though he was much closer in age to Casey than her parents. Casey confused her feelings of love and hate for Peter, but there was always some sort of attraction there. She hadn't thought about him in a long time and he was most distant in her new life and seeing him now was overwhelming to her.

He was handsome, but Randy was more handsome and a stronger person with more substance. They were both terribly charming and a lot alike, but Randy's strengths outweighed Peter's. Randy could be trusted and depended upon. Peter was not real stable. He was also a selfish bastard. He was fun and he did teach Casey a lot about how to handle a man, and Peter always loved Casey and was so physically attracted to her, but she knew she could never live with him. It was so unrealistic, he wasn't the kind of man that she needed to keep her happy forever. There really isn't a man that can keep you happy forever, it just doesn't work that way, a woman has to love herself and then everything will fall in place, and the man will be attracted to her forever

Their drinks had arrived and they were able to quickly meet everyone sitting on either side and across from them in the club car. Casey was really hoping that even though Peter had seen her and made eye contact with her, all unbeknownst to Randy, that would be as far as it would go.

Casey would have been dreaming to think that Peter Munson would just pass through the club car without a polite acknowledgment. She was sipping on her drink and talking with Randy and the people to the right of her when she noticed Peter standing in a navy sport jacket which he probably had made in London, gray trousers and a sparkling white shirt, always monogrammed, at the cuff and a yellow polka dot tie. His sandy blond hair, piercing green eyes and five-foot-ten physique which always appeared taller. He was quite helpless though, but so rich. How Casey wished that he wasn't about to walk her way and even worse than that, join them.

Peter had always been present in her life, she would remember from the day she was born, if she could. She had never been able to forget what a joyous event it was because, in fact, nobody would ever let her. Peter being Daddy's friend, probably remembered this too, even though he was only ten at the time, but his parents lived near Casey's in Winneka and it was strange that business drew him to Ralph's expertise in the tax field, especially due to the fact that a great deal of his business was cash.

Casey always wondered about the connection but it was perfectly obvious, friends, small community and Ralph was top in his field, and Peter having such a huge financial burden on him, especially being an heir to his father's fortune, needed the best.

2

There was always something missing in Peter's life, even though he did know who he was. Maybe it was that he didn't like who he was. He claimed he didn't spend enough time in his mother's womb. His life was so well planned out. He did need someone to take care of him, this was his weakness. He had many personality changes. He hated his mother, Casey thought for a minute. Randy also hated his mother (oh). It had to be the generation, this doesn't have to happen. Randy hated his mother because she was always sick and couldn't be with him, and Peter hated his mother because she never had time for him and he blamed his moodiness on having to be born prematurely and not having been in his mother's womb long enough.

Peter had flashed through Casey's life many times and her first recollection was when he arrived at the Lewis's one snowy Saturday afternoon in December with his mother to see Margaret. Casey, who was having her third birthday party and not thrilled with the whole thing, because Johnny Benton had just pulled her pigtails and bit her on the arm, opened the door to see Peter and his mother standing there. Even though Casey was not sure why she was staring at them and was not even sure if she was glad to see them and was too young to ask them properly to come in, so she stared at them for a while until Margaret realized that they were at the door. She yelled at Casey and said, "Casey, you must not stand there. Ask the Munsons to come in. Whenever you answer the door you must always ask the person in if you know them. Peter chuckled and Casey was torn with staying with the Munsons to playing with her friends.

It was such a joyous and long-awaited event, what a blessing when Peggy and Ralph Lewis gave birth to Casey in the middle years of their lives.

Ralph was prospering as an attorney and powerfully connected in politics. It was a great combination, having social and political influence, and along with power came prestige and influence in controlling some of the most powerful minds of the underworld. It was nothing to come to Ralph for "a favor," and his friends enjoyed socializing with governors, senators, the Vice President of the U.S. and even gangsters. He was well connected in Las Vegas.

In 1942, the United states had joined forces and was well into World War II. This was just after the bombing of Pearl Harbor. Roosevelt was in office, troops were coming home -- there was hope. Factories were starting to flourish again and the automotive industry was coming back. There was this moment in time, the population boom was producing a new generation of independence. Jesus freaks, hippies, yuppies, the baby boomer generation a whole new wave of thought.

Randy was at summer camp in Maine. Prices were on the rise, factory jobs were more available, and Margaret was having a difficult time replacing her couple who had done domestic work for eight years and helped her through the trauma and joys of coping with Casey's arrival. It was always a trauma to replace one's servants, especially since they were so supportive and helpful. With vomiting, night feedings and all of the quirks that take the fun out of raising children.

Casey flourished as a child, being doted upon by everyone; uncles, aunts, her grandmother, parents' friends, cousins, the grocer, the pharmacist, everyone knew Casey, and Casey had an answer for everything. She was precocious and also curtsied when she was introduced to someone for the first time, a sweet protégé. What a wonderful, beautiful child, and Daddy's girl.

It was almost as if she were just a little different than the rest of her friends. She was different. She was partied and wined and dined constantly, whether it was with her parents and their friends, or with other children, it was quite extravagant. She was the envy when she was growing up, even though she didn't always feel that way. Often she loathed her position and often rebelled, wishing she were someone else and sometimes wondering who she was. Was she really Casey? Or Margaret and Ralph's darling daughter, or some little girl who wondered if she would ever grow up into her own person and function without Mommy, Daddy, Aunt Evelyn, Uncle Robert, Cornelia or Mona, her dog. She never wanted her children to be like this. It wasn't normal. It also held her back. She wanted more for her children. Your children should be a better extension of yourself (or at least as good). Casey didn't have to worry because she was "taken care of" and she was thankful for that. She would learn that she was her best friend and the only one she could truly depend on, especially when Ralph died.

Until this time, she gaily floated through childhood doing the usual things that children from affluent families in Winneka, Illinois Beverly Hills, Scarsdale or Shaker Heights. She graduated from New Treer High School in 1960, which put her in the sixties generation: Swing, Chuck Berry, the Beatles, Hippies, Drugs, Campus Riots, Kennedy's Assassination, Woodstock, Rock Concerts, but she still related very strongly to old guard tradition, probably because her parents were older and established, and she missed being victimized by the fifties and having life be over at 40. She went to the proper dance classes, ballroom dancing, the proper nursery schools, the proper summer camps. She was finished properly, but something was missing. Could it have been a sibling to fight with, or the fact that everything was always done for her and maybe she was lacking a certain motivation which was no fault of Margaret or Ralph, they just didn't think about things like this. They had no reason to even direct their thoughts to motivation when they raised Casey. Certain problems or neuroses do not surface until many years past childhood. Casey hated the fact that everything was done for her, she hated being so clean.

Casey was twelve years old now, still being heavily doted on by Margaret and Ralph. Now it was becoming a bit of a strain, especially when Anne had talked of petting and necking with Casey and other friends, Sandy and Madeline. This was a little over Casey's head, but she was certainly able to comprehend it.

The summer that she and her family moved to Sharidan Boulevard, Casey's friends were all older than her. She felt so different than they did. There was something that did separate them, even though they were all the best of friends. Casey was different. She was younger and just starting adolence.

She was finally allowed to go to overnight camp and actually live away from Margaret and Ralph for the first time since birth. Her friend Sally had begged her to go, and her mother convinced Casey's mother that it would be a good experience, and, knowing how much Casey wanted to go, her mother thought it would be fine since they knew Sally's family from the club.

Along with Sally that summer, they were joined by their third best friend, Suzy, who introduced Casey to a drag on a cigarette and padded bras. It helped, anything helped, to add a little sophistication to her body, which was flat as a pancake, solid like a rock and fully packed. Daddy was right, though, she thought, she did have gorgeous legs. Casey also met two more good friends which formed a nucleus for their crowd in junior high. Karen was all caught up in being beautiful and Elizabeth was just fucked up and she didn't know it.

Camp was a very positive experience. In fact, it made Casey really realize how much she enjoyed being away from home and from Margaret and Ralph. It was the first time that she had really ever felt a real feeling about herself all by herself. They all loved camp and made new friends too, except for Elizabeth, who loathed it, and kept very much to herself and didn't seem to want to be part of the group. She was different. This was not a good experience for her. Did she miss her parents?

This was after the Korean War. Fashion of the fifties was fabulous, full skirts, tight pants, high heels, tight fitting suits even showing more skin on beaches. Virgin marriages were still very much in style. Elvis Presley was a smash and Sam Shephard killed his wife Marilyn, all in the same summer that Casey was at camp.

Randy was married. He had two children and was totally committed to his family business. He was the heir apparent and working his way fast to the top of a five-generation-old manufacturing business of designer apparel. Calvin Kline as a name of the seventies, but David Alan was very established in the fifties as the largest manufacturer of sweaters and sportswear in the Midwest. David Alan was a tradition.

3

Casey had just come back to the bunk from swimming dripping wet and the sweet scent of candy permeated Bunk C. If Thack, their counselor, caught on, they would all be in big trouble because she was very strict with the Pandas, which were the 13 to 14 year olds. Elizabeth came into Casey's bunk very tearful because her mother and father just left; it was parents visiting weekend. Casey actually felt relief that her mother had gone. Her father didn't make the trip because Margaret was worried about his heart and in the mid-fifties, it was considered a strenuous trip to visit camp in Maine.

Casey was glad to see her mother but quite undisturbed when she departed. Folly Pittman also stopped by the bunk to see if she could borrow some comic books, and although Casey couldn't spend too much time with her because Elizabeth was in a manic distraught state, she was able to tip Folly off about the candy and told her to try to get back before taps because Thacker was on kitchen and O.D. that night. Folly loved candy and she would do anything for it. It didn't even show on her; however, Casey was always fighting fat. Margaret had her at the diet table, which was beneficial because she was growing and developing into a beautiful young girl, and she was able to trim down some of her baby fat at the same time.

Camp was definitely the start of Casey's long friendship with Folly, who was one of the best friends she had in spite of their differences.

Casey was feminine and beautiful and kind and loving, and Folly, who had a harder life, was tough, almost butch dyke like, irrational at times, and had a very low self-esteem. She was a very jealous and mean person, but somehow their differences worked. Folly always envied Casey, and admired her, although Casey never thought about that and overlooked Folly's shortcomings because Casey also admired something about her and for Casey it was easy to have her as a friend because she didn't have to give a lot, and she admired her independence. Casey always attracted Folly's men for her and Folly probably never appreciated that or how Casey really always loved and looked out for her because they were such good friends. Folly was evil and jealous and she just could not help herself. She was also a self-centered bitch and she never matured or outgrew this; she only became more bitter. Their friendship was more than a friendship, it was a relationship shared through sickness, love, marriage, death, divorce, and most of all life. Even though they weren't related, they both agreed that they were the closest thing to sisters, and while they knew each other at camp, they never dreamed that their paths would cross throughout life and they would become very close friends. Although she was from Lexington, Kentucky, which was a small town near southern Ohio, their paths did cross because as Casey, her family, was well connected socially and they met in Chicago when Folly moved there for the summer to work at Marshall Field, which was her uncle's store. Casey was best friends with Folly's cousin, Lisa, and of course she was immediately introduced to Folly.

Folly and Casey remembered and reminisced about camp, the Lions and Tigers; they were both team captains. Folly had also taken as great a liking for men as she had for the scent of candy in Bunk C. This was a subject about which Casey was still very naive, even though she had experienced several dating relationships. Folly was sent to Chicago to get away from the fast life she was living at UCLA and in Beverly Hills. Her exposure to drugs and sex in the sixties was far beyond anything that Casey or Lisa or Elizabeth and Sally from camp days would even fantasize about, and at this time in her life, Folly looked her best. Young and beautiful and healthy.

Having never gone all the way until her freshman year at Stanford, which was only two years before her marriage to Barry Brickman, who came from the "right" family and had the approval of Casey's parents, Peggy and Ralph Rothchild, she was rather naive and inexperienced, especially in the sixties when there was so much emphasis on sexual freedom, because this was an independent time before the AIDS virus, and having to be careful only if you didn't want to get pregnant.

Casey had a few boyfriends and of course she had fallen in love with the wrong boy at Stanford and she would never marry without her parents' approval.

She was now in a crowd with Sally's sister Barbara, who was older, and of course Casey and her friends at that time looked up to her and idolized her.

Barbara always found the girls dates and it was a tight little clique. There were only two or three suitable men in Chicago to date at this time, and Casey knew that Sally, Elizabeth and Karen were all unconsciously pursuing them because they had already realized that high school boys were out and even a grade or two ahead was not right. Barry was actually the youngest in the crowd. But did she really know what love was, and even though Casey was unaware at the time, there were subtle pressures from her parents. Why hadn't she taken a grip on the whole situation? Was she really too immature mentally? Maybe even physically. Although at twenty, she was approaching actual adulthood, how depressing, or maybe this was all part of the journey and the most exciting start to realizing she was taking charge of her life.

Her life would have been much different had she dealt with all of these situations. Maybe she should have had someone to discuss this with, but did she really know what was happening? Of course not, and she would have never met Randy if she had really thought about what she was doing with herself at twenty.

4

Many years have passed and Casey was developing into a beautiful woman, leaving behind the baby fat that she fought throughout her childhood. She was, in fact, much more beautiful than she ever dreamed that she was, very sensuous and not conscious of the fact that she had an inborn way about her when it came to handling men and knowing how to treat them. She had a wonderful innocence about her and this became her most obscure feature in knowing how to treat a man. She also learned later that this intuition also served not only in the handling of a man, which could be qualified as prey, but in handling creatures of the same sex. Whether she picked this trait up from her father or not, it was there, and she was a great manipulator of people, which would prove to be a great defense mechanism to her eventually.

Peter Munson, who had evaporated from Casey's life for many years for one reason or another, suddenly appeared around Chicago. Actually, she couldn't really recall seeing him much after she met him at her birthday party, but he had left a big impression on her, because her thoughts would often be on Peter, even though they were fantasies. Casey had no interest that there could ever be any kind of attraction between the two except maybe a supportive friendship, which had been a little one-sided on Casey's part. Anything to do with Peter seemed quite unrealistic to Casey since their lives were going in different directions.

Casey was a nice girl going to Stanford, and studying very hard to pursue a career. She had everything going for the right person to grab. Peter was spoiled, and difficult, and going from one woman to the next. This was not what Margaret had pictured for Casey. He did have a lot of money, but everything else, according to Margaret, was terrible. He drank, and partied, and they had even heard rumors of orgies that were going on at his country estate.

Of course, even Casey herself could admit that he was a handsome man, but what trouble. Casey even admitted care of Folly that she would love to marry a prince someday, but it would never be Peter Munson. Casey and Folly often thought, why do men have to be so involved in themselves all the time. Casey knew that she didn't want her life to be unreal, and she did know that she wanted a man whose interest was involved in her intellect. Not just in achieving sexual gratification. Men could be such schmucks.

Casey was beginning to think that all men were essentially the same, even Randy had some of these chauvinistic traits. Could it be the male animal? Casey had even noticed it in young men, but it could be that they were like that because they imitated their fathers. If the child finds someone that they can relate to or identify with in a situation like that, a new father image, they will turn out to be a stronger personality and it could have a positive impact on the child. Only children have very strong identities, which could be attributed to the fact that they have no sibling rivalry. They also have a great deal of confidence, not having to deal with sibling rivalry.

Why did Peter have to be on the Orient Express? Casey had learned as she grew wiser with age and with the challenges that she had to deal with, that 'why' was forbidden in her vocabulary unless she wanted to deal with the crazies and the deep psychological factors involved. When something happens in a person's life, you certainly can cause yourself a lot of pain and trauma by always searching for unanswered questions. It can be exhausting and cause you more grief than humanly bearable. It is much more feasible to question the present into the future and the conclusion is to see the answer for the end result that you are putting so much time and energy into.

Peter was on the train and Casey burned when she looked at him. Randy was oblivious to all of this. However, the tension created by the two being in the same room together was apparent to others around them. Casey thought to herself, maybe she should be so angry, maybe she was burning with anger at Randy because he wasn't paying any attention to what was happening, and why should she let herself feel guilty at the sight of Peter? Should she be filled with anger at Randy? Casey's emotions were so confused right now, but she was just going to let it happen. She sipped her drink and chatted with Randy about the beauty of the train and the children.

Peter made his way over to them. They were both cordial and polite, Casey more so than Randy. She was glad that she didn't have to go through certain social amenities because they did already know each other through clubs, business and mutual acquaintances.

Casey could uncomfortably feel Peter moving closer to her and paying a great deal more attention to her than was really necessary. There was a synergy between them. It wasn't even very flattering, but you know how it is when you have something you don't really want, and when you don't have it, you really long for it. Life is so strange.

She was concerned about Randy. He had a terrible temper and a very dark side to him, and he could be physically violent. Casey was careful and certainly didn't want to cause a scene, not in the club car.

Conversation was going quite well and they had formed a group of people which became the nucleus of the club car, their crowd, which would eventually continue to dinner. Casey couldn't believe the whole thing and Randy was being such a gentleman. She was happy.

Peter as not a part of Casey's life that she was proud of. She was very immature when she met him and didn't have control of herself as a person. She was also being pursued by Barry Brickman, who was nice, with the proper credentials. He was, actually, too nice, but he turned into a schmuck, a real wimp. Casey knew that she needed more than a nice boy, but her parents were not aware of this. Actually, this was something that was never discussed. There was something a little odd about Barry, but she learned to accept it.

This was a deal that Casey made to herself after Barry's death; life is too short and too precious, and never settle for anything that isn't the way that you want it to be. Casey probably did this quite often subconsciously, not meaning to hurt anyone.

Peter aggressively pursued Casey while she was going with Barry. It was a very confusing time for her. She liked Peter in a very guarded way, because she knew he was capable of hurting her, and with Barry, she felt comfortable, secure and superior. It wasn't right, though. Peter was fun, but she knew that she must not see him and she must concentrate on her life with Barry.

This was building up all the right ingredients for finding Randy. Meeting Randy was the fulfillment of Casey's dreams and fantasies. He seemed right for her at this time, he turned her on. He was handsome. He had money. He loved her.

It wasn't fair, though, because Peter and Barry became friends. How low. How was Casey going to tolerate this? She knew that she wouldn't be happy with Peter, but at twenty, she would have a shot at happiness with Barry. What Casey didn't know was that Barry was a paranoid schizophrenic, which would change her life drastically. Peter was the kind of person who didn't like to take no for an answer, but Casey only had no's for him and couldn't think of including him in anything positive in her life. He was the kind of man that women could grow to hate. What a shame, because he really could have a lot to offer.

Casey and Barry were quite happy and planning to be married. It was very social and very proper and, of course, they took a three-month honeymoon around the world. There were lavish parties given for the couple before the wedding and they were married in the garden of Ralph and Margaret's home. It was quite an event and famous people were invited from all over the world for the wedding. Ralph had many political friends there. Richard Nixon and movie stars came in, and Frank Sinatra, who was an old friend, along with friends, relatives and business associates.

Peter, that schmuck, managed to have himself invited to be in the wedding party. What nerve. He was stalking her, harassing her. Casey could not get rid of him. If she asked herself, psychologically, if she wanted to get rid of him, that could be a difficult question to answer. She was able to introduce him to one of her friends, Nicole, that would take the pressure off of her for a while, maybe even forever.

It was a hot July evening and Casey was dressing to go to a black tie affair that was being given in honor of her marriage to Barry at the Munsons. Casey's dress was exquisite. Margaret had found it at Neiman Marcus and it was a champagne lace cocktail length, off the shoulder dress. Casey's skin looked especially lovely tonight. It could have been the complement of the color she was wearing.

Barry arrived a little early at the Munsons' party since it was being given in their honor. The house was gorgeous, beautifully decorated for the party. The tables all looked as if they belonged in a French garden. Casey could only think that this was more than a friendship, it had to be a business friendship because the party was so opulent.

Peter Duchin played along with an orchestra that was flown in from New York. Everybody looked absolutely gorgeous. Every famous designer was represented: Dior, St. Laurent, Chanel, Galanos, Mackie, Oscar De LaRenta This was the event. Casey felt a surging sensation move through her body because she was a guest at her own party and she would actually be able to enjoy it too. The wedding would be anti-climactic after this, but so what.

Barry was charming and Casey attentive, but something still told her that something was missing. She was so young and naive and could only rationalize that it would get better. Peter had his eye on her and she was just intoxicated with life, love and happiness enough tonight to be drawn to Peter's convincing line of bullshit. Again the fantasies flashed through Casey's mind, and they were all sexual fantasies.

Only this time, Peter led Casey into the garden and slowly started to undress her partially clad body. The sensation was erotic, Casey's skin tingled and she quivered with Peter's every touch.

Casey couldn't take it. She blinked her eyes so she could face reality and get back to the party. Only then, when Peter asked Casey to dance, and she did, of course, not wanting to be rude. How could he be so aggressive here, tonight. This was ridiculous, and now, before her wedding, it was absurd, but Peter was so persistent. Casey thought a bit to herself. She was flattered by this and was rather enjoying the whole thing, not even concerned about Barry at this moment.

Casey had had several premarital relationships, which was perfectly normal for an attractive young woman of her age. Casey knew that she loved sex, and she also knew that she wanted to indulge herself in many different forms of gratification. It was the 70's, a time of love and sexual freedom. It was something which she really enjoyed and made her feel good, and she knew that she was great at it. She wasn't at all afraid, either. The only hang-up that she had was that Ralph and Margaret had always preached that "nice girls don't."

Casey never analyzed her affairs or relationships. She didn't think that she was being rebellious, she really did enjoy herself. It made her feel free and independent. She remembered when she had her first experience, which really was like nothing. It was almost anti-climactic because of the fear she had of losing her virginity, which undoubtedly had gone somewhere along the way at camp or through some sort of athletic activity, such as horseback riding. However, Casey did recall that she did enjoy the sexual encounters that she had and wasn't searching, but she knew she needed to experience more. The apptitude and lust and sensitivity were all there. Casey wasn't really ready for marriage but she was getting a great deal of peer pressure.

Casey and Peter danced and then disappeared into the garden. Casey knew that she had control of the situation but she could feel that she would be losing it soon, and she didn't even care. Peter had managed to take a glass of champagne with him and they toasted, drank, and defied all the rules. This was bizarre. Casey had unrelentlessly given herself, unforsaken, wholly, to Peter Munson, not thinking of what kind of effect this would have and her future. It was madness.

They had been gone from the party too long and although the party was big enough, she was the guest of honor and she would be missed. Eventually, Casey knew that she must blank out this experience from her mind and that she could not continue to see Peter. Peter begged Casey not to go through with her marriage to Barry, but she was not able to think about this now. What had she done? The timing was all wrong. She had to pretend that this never happened and go on with her life. Peter had no right interfering. Now the timing was the worst and this angered her terribly and made her resent Peter. Throughout her relationship with Randy, and they did have their ups and downs, she did not ever remember being so angry. How was Casey going to go back to the party and face her guests and Barry? She would have to do it!

As Peter and Casey walked into the party, they chatted with some of the guests and then with Barry and eventually his parents. It was all so easy and Casey was able to forget the guilt that she suffered with Peter. She was even able to start enjoying the party that was being given for her and in addition to that, she felt a tinge of excitement rush through her body as she danced with Barry and thought of where she had just come from. It was exciting and it was Casey's first awareness that she loved action, excitement and the fast track. This experience, the interplay between the guests, was a high to her. Nobody was aware of this except Casey, and this could be rebellious immaturity. It was wrong, but so right for Casey. It was a high.

Peter was so charming to Casey, but she felt and acted quite embarrassed. She was overcome by guilt every time she looked at Barry, and her only rationale was that she was not married. This wasn't something that she could discuss with Ralph. His viewpoint on life was just too different from hers and he might think she had gone crazy. Ralph was just too provincial to discuss this with.

If Casey had been in this situation now, especially after all that she had experienced after Barry's mental collapse, she would have taken this to her doctor, but Casey just thought about it or would try to erase it from her life and go on with what was important.

She did meet Douglas Remington for a drink and they always had a good laugh, and she was able to really confide in him about herself. Of course, she never dreamed that he had been lusting for her in spite of a very platonic relationship. Douglas was so handsome, in his own way, and kind and so witty. His sense of humor was marvelous. His charm and good looks actually came from within his personality because although he was so lovable, there wasn't a whole lot to love in his five-foot/ten physique but his thick, curly hair, added to his virility, he was superb and his mind was absolutely phenomenal, and boring was not a state of mind for him. They always had a great time when they were together, and actually, Casey could thank Douglas for teaching her a great deal about men and how to treat them.

She started to tell Douglas of her predicament, not really thinking that he was more than interested in her situation. With Peter, he was actually stimulated from it. Douglas immediately helped rid Casey of her guilt and had her thinking for herself and living for herself. She felt so much better. Douglas was overwrought by the sexual encounter in the garden and encouraged Casey to continue seeing Peter because he was sure that she did not achieve the maximum pleasure from a somewhat rushed experience which had to be more satisfying for Peter. Douglas was such a devil, he was actually coaxing Casey to continue seeing Peter. She kept saying to Douglas that she couldn't because the guilt was too great and that she suffered, and he would dissuade her from all these feelings.

Casey did feel herself becoming stronger and she began to think for herself and not have to depend on friends and relatives for important decisions that had to be made in her life. Folly Newhouse helped her think for herself, whether she was aware of that or not, because Casey would ask Folly certain things that she was troubled with and Folly would make her come to her own conclusion, and then they would discuss the pros and cons. Folly helped Casey know herself and how she looked good so that she wouldn't have to depend on others for gratification. Casey thought Folly was the strongest person she knew, but she was also one of the weakest. Folly was the most self-destructive of all of her friends and obtuse.

5

Every hour of every day was filled with things that revolved around the wedding. It was exasperating. Casey was going from fittings to parties, to showers, lunches, brunches, and finding out that she was tired and even irritable. It didn't seem to bother her parents or Barry's, they seemed to be enjoying the parties and, of course, this was probably the most excitement that Florence had ever derived from her marriage to Max. Not only were they able to attend the best parties, but it was a super opportunity for them to social climb, which they loved to do.

Peter had been calling and Casey was not accepting phone calls because she was so busy and exhausted. The wedding was getting closer and the pressure great. Barry had to go out of town with his dad on business, and the Rothschilds went to the club for dinner with Florence. In the middle of dinner, Peter appeared and joined them. Casey and Peter chatted so naturally and, in fact, Peter was good company to Casey in this situation, which was becoming a little intolerable.

What balls Peter had. He asked Casey, in front of her family, if she would like to go to a movie with him. It seemed like a perfectly lovely idea to Ralph because he was getting ready to retire for the night, have a brandy, watch some television and get ready for bed.

Peter took Casey home. They went to a movie and stopped at Peter's on their way home. This was no fantasy, it was really happening. Now Peter and Casey knew that they both wanted each other, feeling the driving force to be close to each other. They quietly walked back into the formal gardens at the Munsons, knowing that they couldn't take the chance of being caught together. Casey remained wrapped around Peter as he started from her lips to kiss her in every crevice of her beautifully formed body. Her legs became so weak that before she realized where she was, she was kneeling at Peter with her head buried in his knees. Peter and she had started undressing each other and planting wet kisses all over each other. Casey seemed to know just what to do to please him. She touched every derivative point on Peter. She had him in her power. Casey responded to everything that Peter did to her. Peter loved her.

Barry was coming home tomorrow and she could not believe that she had lost her head over Peter. She had to regain her composure. She hadn't even slept with Barry and all that Casey could think about was how wet she became with Peter, and how much they loved kissing each other. Casey knew that she loved to fuck. Having had a very sheltered life and only having one premarital experience before Peter, she never thought about it that much, but now she knew.

Barry was expected back in town and Casey thought this would be an ideal time to make him welcome. She had to forget Peter, he was just filling space. He was a dysfunctional human being, gorgeous and loving, but he didn't have the strength and stability that she needed.

Barry was glad to see Casey and actually only his mother's domination had stopped him from totally possessing her before now, along with his guilt that he was so inbred. Barry seemed satisfied and content and Casey accepted the sexual act graciously. This was right, she thought. This was the sweetness. Casey had only been in love and turned on by her first love in college. Ned and she hadn't experimented enough with sex to know what she really needed. Barry would be a good husband and they would have a good life, and her parents would be happy.

6

The wedding was spectacular, and Margaret spared nothing since this was the only time that she would be putting on a production like this. Casey made it beautifully through the wedding, even in spite of the fact that Peter was part of the wedding party. Casey made a pact with herself that Peter was just a friend and that she could not interfere in that friendship.

Life for Casey went well. They lived well, traveled well, and outside of very mundane little things, they were happy and were also very much envied by friends. John and Leslye were born, Barry's business was prospering. The children were both beautiful and healthy and John, especially, exhibited a strong personality from birth. He was very precocious and Leslye, too, was just beautiful, easy going and very bright and receptive. They were beautiful children, John, very masculine and handsome, and Leslye was a gorgeous blue-eyed blonde with perfect features. Leslye worked hard to achieve what she wanted and always seemed to accomplish that. She was a beauty and used all of her assets. She was driven and powerful, like Casey.

The Viet Nam vets were coming home. The Beatles had risen to fame and were starting to individualize themselves. A man by the name of Elton John was dancing on pianos and displaying much talent, and women were breaking away from duties of the home and entering the work force in the same capacities as men. Students were rioting on college campuses. High-powered drugs were being used. Tripping on L.S.D. in the 70's was like beer and scotch in the 50's.

Barry enjoyed being a father and seemed especially close to John. Leslye, who was just born shortly before his breakdown, was an absolute beauty. She had gorgeous blue eyes and blonde hair and was exquisite from the moment of birth.

Barry was so happy and elated that he had the nursery redecorated. He bought Casey lavish gifts and he really seemed to have his life totally under control.

Casey and Barry were just thrilled with the children. They were enjoying their beautiful new house, loved the children. Barry was prospering in business. The only thing they regretted was that Ralph's death had robbed them of the opportunity to share all this happiness with him. It also took the strength that Barry needed to identify with and function.

Barry, who had lived marginally because of Max's propensity for frugality, was buying expensive foreign cars, spending money on himself, traveling and living a completely different life style. Casey and the children were all a wonderful part of this life. Leslye and John were developing a strong identity for their parents and each moment with them was precious and recorded on film or in photographs.

Casey's nurse was staying with Leslye for two months to help with both children and to give Barry and Casey a chance to get away for a couple of weeks by themselves. Barry had made plans for the Dominican Republic because he heard about a great resort there and thought it would be good for them to get away.

Casey was excited and she had always liked traveling with Barry, they always met interesting people.

Prior to the nervous breakdown, Barry began to show some symptoms of withdrawal. The truth was that he needed to get away from business and his father. The pressures that were so great to him were not money or business pressures, but fthe thought of spending the rest of his life working for Max and running Maxco Industries. This was a very depressing thought to Barry, unbeknownst to Casey. It had to do with Barry's identity with Max, his father.

It was quite sad to Casey that Ralph didn't get to live to see Leslye and a loss that was taken even deeper by Barry due to the fact that he was not well, even though no one was aware of it at this time.

Casey knew that her dad was a powerful figure, but never dreamed that his strength really held Barry together. It did.

Barry was under pressure because he wanted a change in his life. When all of this surfaced, Casey was willing to go along with what he wanted, thinking it might help his condition. Randy understood this when he met her and was very compassionate and understanding to her situation because he had experienced this with members of his immediate family, and it gave Casey great strength and stability to know that she could relate her feelings to someone after Ralph's death, who was genuinely concerned and who really understood. Casey thought a trip at this time was a bit extravagant, but Barry insisted.

Margaret's health was failing. She was having severe lapses of memory since Ralph's death. Her heart was failing too, and her doctors told Casey that it was just a matter of time for her and that surgery was out of the question for her problem. This was very depressing to Casey. Margaret seemed to enjoy the children most in her life and they seemed to bring her great pleasure. This was comforting to Casey during this difficult time with her mother. They were the only happiness in Margaret's life.

Casey and Barry left for the Dominican Republic, leaving the children in excellent hands with Lilli Rose and Nursey Potter.

It was the middle of the night and Barry had appeared back at his room at the Regency Hotel in New York City. He was missing for almost a week and Casey was stranded in the Dominican Republic at Casa del Campo, trying to keep her sanity by getting a lot of rest and keeping in touch with guests at the resort as well as the manager of the hotel so she might be able to hear some news about Barry.

It came as a great shock to everyone when the family was notified that Barry was in New York and not quite himself, and that he had been wandering aimlessly for almost a week in New York City. Casey, in the Dominican Republic, could hardly get communications to her family or Barry's, and she was so helpless and terribly worried about the children because she could not reach her family. She was so frustrated, and could turn to nobody for help. Florence and Max were stunned and offered little emotional support to anyone. They were very selfish and cold people and did not know how to give of themselves.

Casey's parents would have been enraged because they were never told of any of Barry's previous mental breakdowns when he was in college. This was a mess and Casey was so young to cope with so much. Margaret was the only person that Casey could turn to and she was in terribly failing health since Ralph's death and really not aware of what was really happening, as she did not know what was going on with her own illness or herself.

Barry's parents were cold, insensitive people who could not focus beyond themselves. If Ralph had been alive he would have been at Casey's side in this foreign country or certainly would have sent help to her. She had more than just Barry's problem. She couldn't get medical help and there was a language barrier. Either Florence and Max were so selfish and insensitive, or they were too stupid and narrow-minded to know what to do, and they couldn't function past the shock, and Casey had to do it all.

Barry had left Casey without money and credit cards. She didn't know how she was even going to check out of the hotel and get home. Casey's only communication while she was there was with natives and Americans at the hotel, which was limited. Barry had disappeared. He was tripping on his own highs or drugs given to him by people he was with. He was in a bad state of mind.

He appeared at the hotel and Casey was able to convince him at lunch, and it was hard because he was in a hyperactive state of mind, to give her the plane tickets so she could return to Chicago and check herself out of the hotel. A friend that she made at the hotel accompanied her to the airport. Barry was off again and later Casey heard that he had flown to Morocco and finally checked into the Regency Hotel in New York with no shoes on his feet.

Casey was able to make it back to Chicago and there she was notified of Barry's whereabouts in New York City. She barely kissed the children and early the next morning she and Barry's parents were on their way to New York. Casey called her attorney, who flew in because she knew she couldn't bear to be in Florence and Max's company without him.

New York was intense, with psychiatrists and committing Barry to a 'safe' hospital so he wouldn't end up at Bellevue, which would be more than beneficial. This was the hardest thing that Casey had ever gone through in her life. It was like living on the outside and watching yourself go through this horrible experience, and to see Barry like this was very hard. But he did have his highs and his lows. This was like a nightmare. It was an adventure. Who would ever believe it? Casey even had difficulty at times.

Casey was angry that this was happening to Barry and that she couldn't help him. And she was angry that his past history of mental illness had never been discussed with her before. And the most disturbing thing to her was the effect this would have on the children and the stability of a solid family life. She wasn't depressed but she did feel trapped.

It was also very difficult for Casey because she didn't have anyone to turn to about her problems.

Since Ralph's death, Casey matured a lot. She learned to take care of many situations that confronted her and she was able to accept many challenges. She also learned that if you want to accomplish something, you do it yourself. Margaret was too ill to be of any support to Casey. She had developed a disease which was diagnosed as pulmonary hypertension. There were many similarities between Barry and her mother, even though one illness was mental and one physical. Casey had no idea that Randy would end up with Alzheimer's disease and how lucky she would be to have been divorced from him. It was almost kind of like her revenge, but that is being vicious (tongue in cheek), as she really didn't wish what was going to happen to him or anyone.

7

Casey was so young and sheltered, having been raised by Margaret and Ralph who always took care of everything for her. Ralph was very ill with heart failure and this added to the pressure that Casey had to deal with Margaret, who always did everything for everyone, was not acting normally, nor could she remember what she was doing from one day to the next, but she was able to cover this up very well. Casey had no idea how ill she was.

Florence and Max were only interested in themselves, and they were not any comfort or help to the situation. They could hardly lend any help to Casey as to how to deal with Barry She was facing her problems and had pretty good control of the situation, but Barry's parents were the most peculiar people. There was no doubt that Barry's problems were manifested by the coldness, insecurity and lack of love and understanding that he received from his parents.

Casey could never quite understand the relationship. Was it that they were selfish, or that they had very confused values and that to them family did not mean what it means to most or to Casey -- family was a first priority. Nevertheless, the relationship that Casey witnessed between Barry and his parents was strange. It was painful for Casey to experience Barry's rejection and know that all she could do for Barry was to try to understand him and try to be a helpful force, because he did need it. He felt so persecuted. Casey was very nice to Barry throughout his illness. She thought very little of herself and her own gratification, even though her doctors encouraged her to put herself first and take care of her own needs.

She also tried to build up his confidence and self-esteem, which was something that his family had no sensitivity to. Barry was paranoid at times, docile, sometimes very energetic, and feeling very persecuted, that's why he always looked to make friends and be with friends. It was very painful to suffer acute persecution. He felt beaten down and alone, and his self-esteem was low.

Barry had no business being discharged from the hospital, not in the condition that he was in, especially after having spent a week in total confinement and hardly uttering a word to anyone. This was the most difficult part of Barry's illness for Casey. It destroyed her to see him in this environment. It was also during this period that Casey faced the true reality that Barry was seriously ill and that this was a chronic situation over which she had no control.

Casey had experienced throughout Barry's illness tremendous highs, but he was in the depths of depression. Now, the cause was undetermined. The only thing that his doctors could establish for sure was that this condition could be a chemical imbalance. It was also diagnosed as paranoid schizophrenia.

Casey shuddered when she heard the words. She only wanted Barry to get better and be able to function with her normally. She only wanted the children to have a normal life. What a curse this was.

Casey had witnessed a secret of her father's when she was a little girl and it was something that stayed with her until her mid-life. Her father, Ralph, was dead, and she still could not talk about the secret.

Casey had been through so much, so much more than her other friends, that made her independent, strong, and a very free-thinking person. Her experiences in life had made her grow and made her age like a fine wine.

She was very unique, coming from a fine upper-class background. Being the only child of a very powerful businessman had also made her strong and confident and helped her to be able to deal with life and survive.

This secret touched many people in Casey's life and it wasn't something that surfaced until her fifth decade. She was very fortunate to have been born at a time in history that she was, and probably oblivious to the fact that her father was such a powerful person. To her he was just Daddy.

The secret she witnessed involved senators, a former president and the attorney general. She was worried that John and Lesly's lives could be in danger. There were large amounts of money exchanged between 'very higher ups' in government and the Las Vegas mob, and there were also favors that were being transferred between the two. It would eventually involve cancelled checks from Ralph's office that were destroyed by Mervin, his flunky.

Nobody could understand why he did such a stupid thing at that time, because it could only attract attention from the I.R.S. that nobody was looking for. Mervin even tried to have Barry removed as executor of Ralph's estate on the premise of incompetence, but Casey fought this and won, and Mervin, that bastard, was removed. Barry, as sick mentally as he was, still wasn't satisfied with this decision because he knew Mervin was hiding something and that he was up to no good. This secret would involve Randy, as well. It could also be responsible for some unknown mysteries that occurred, as well as an unsolved murder.

Casey was frantic. She was scared and she didn't know how to react. She was beside herself and she didn't know who to turn to. She was advised to talk to the head of the department about Barry instead of to Dr. Switzer, who was Barry's doctor. He was wonderful and very easy to talk to. He was very sympathetic to her situation. She could relate her innermost feelings about herself to him and it was a great release to her. Casey was able to think about Barry's coming home with her and relax about it and actually cope with the thought of having him in the house.

The decision was made to let Barry come home from the hospital because he was so adamant about wanting to be at home. His doctors thought this would be the best therapy for his depression and if it didn't help, he would go back to the hospital for more treatment.

Casey went to pick up Barry and she was more nervous about seeing him than she had ever been. She had not been eating much and whatever she did eat, did not seem to stay with her very long. She looked beautiful but she was a bundle of nerves inside, and she didn't want Barry to know this.

She hid her emotions beautifully. It was a hot fall day, the sun shone so brightly that it felt like summer. Barry was waiting for Casey to arrive and when he came out to the Mercedes where Casey was waiting with the sun roof open, he looked more handsome than Casey had every remembered him being. He was also very thin and very lucid. His eyes were not glassy as they usually were from all of the medication that he was taking. She hadn't talked to Dr. Switzer about his medication, but maybe he wasn't on any.

He did so well over the weekend that he wanted to stay home for the week. Casey had no objection as he was doing so well. And again, she had hope for his recovery as she had so many times in the past. Thinking about this made her very tearful, because she and the children were living on the edge of a very unstable and unpredictable situation, and as much fun as the great moments that they had together were, the bad moments were unmentionable. It was wonderful being a family again, doing things with the children, opening the house to friends and cooking and cleaning and just mundane, normal things that Casey cherished, loved and appreciated. She was so happy and grateful for Barry's recovery. She hoped and prayed that this time he was really cured. However, with mental illness, that is an unpredictable request.

On Sunday, Douglas and Jennifer stopped over for a visit and Barry seemed to especially enjoy their company. Jennifer was madly in love with Douglas and living with him with hopes of a future. Douglas, Casey's old friend from high school, could be somewhat unpredictable, but Casey only knew that she had an affinity for him. However, she didn't think that it could relate to marriage. They all did have a great time that Sunday. Barry was so relaxed and conversive. Casey served lunch and it was a great afternoon.

Barry wanted to go for a ride, so they all piled into the Mercedes with the children and drove out to the country. They had some super debates over Watergate, great conversation, and Douglas's wit and humor, as always, was superb. After solving world-shaking situations, stopping for ice-cream, and driving, and conversation filled with laughter and tears from the laughter, they drove right to Mr. Wong's and ordered enough Chinese food to feed an army. They decided to wait because Barry was enjoying talking to people that he knew that were also stopping at the restaurant for orders to go. The children should have each gotten gold stars, they were so good. Nobody was even the least bit guarded because of Barry. He was so easy to be with, it was almost too good to be true.

They got back to Barry and Casey's and immediately plunged into the Chinese food. It was a feast.

Douglas was mentioning a litigation that he was working on and Randy Foxman was the owner of one of the parent companies in the case. Douglas was just bringing Barry up to date. It was of interest to Casey because she had missed the article in the newspaper. She was so involved with Barry at the hospital. Douglas also mentioned something about Randy's divorce and his being quite wealthy. This was all of little interest to Casey, especially because she didn't know who they were speaking of or what this would have to do with her and her life.

8

Barry started talking about taking a safari to Africa and it sounded quite exciting. However, Casey neveeeeeeer knew when to take Barry seriously, especially after his last breakdown when he left her in the Dominican Republic alone shortly after Leslye was born. She glanced at Douglas and Jennifer, but they were anxious to hear more about this. It was at times like this that Casey used to feel panicked and it was hard for her to describe these feelings to anybody. Barry was most definite that he had turned upside down. It was shocking and traumatic. Casey found these stories hard to believe. They sounded like lies, and it was very hard for her to listen to them. Furthermore, she could not picture Barry in certain situations that she had heard of. She could not in her wildest imagination picture Barry making love to another woman, not because he was so in love with her. She just could not, somehow, see him in this kind of a situation. He never seemed the type. He was having hallucinations and fantasies about her which he not only told his psychiatrist about, but all of his friends and, of course, a few of them started to come on to Casey. This was just what she didn't need at this particular point in time. However, it would have been a perfect outlet for some of her jealous and horny friends. They were such bitches at times, but she could forgive their frustrations.

Casey could not get through to Barry so the only contact that she had with him was to meet and try to become friendly with people that Barry had met, but he had been travelling at such a fast pace that even that was hard. Sergio Franki, who was entertaining at the hotel, had become quite friendly with Barry. This was the only time that Casey could make any kind of mental contact with him because for some reason when she would just walk into his cabana and sit down and talk to them, Barry would speak to her and they were unbelievably happy and together.

But then the day would end, and Barry would disappear. She would talk to Sergio about Barry and that he needed help, but the whole situation was so bizarre that Sergio probably thought that she was the insane one. Casey found herself confronted a lot with this situation. It was a lack of communication and it was frustrating because she couldn't get help for Barry. He did, however, know that something was wrong. People that Barry was coming in contact with knew that he was crazy.

Barry had been up for nights. He had sores on his feet from walking on the beach, and actually Casey thought he looked pretty well. He was extremely hyperactive. Casey's life was flashing from fantasy to reality and back to fantasy. She was definitely in touch with herself, but she did admit to herself that this episode was filled with excitement, and Casey did love action and excitement. It was living life in the fast lane.

She was very worried about the children who were so young and what kind of a future they would have. She also knew that nothing would interfere with the welfare and raising of Leslye and John. And she knew that right now they were in good hands with Nursey Potter and Lily Rose.

Casey knew that her primary concern was to be with Barry and to try to reach him. This was the most difficult thing that Casey had ever done. She actually had to handle Barry because in a sense he was rejecting her and not wanting to communicate with her. Casey being very smart for her years, met these challenges and was able to cope with dealing with Barry and his split personality. It was love, hate, love, hate, reality, fantasy. Casey often thought to herself she liked the fantasies better than the realities. What was she going to do? She had nobody on this trip to turn to that seemed stable or somewhat trustworthy, so she began to act on her own instincts and sensitivity.

She was able to communicate with one man at the hotel who seemed fairly stable and wasn't a musician or a member of a rock group. The important thing about this contact was that he was able to build up a rapport with Barry and act as a go between. Mark Pomerantz was very helpful to Casey and she was able to deal with this time in her life that was totally unrealistic much better. Mark was able to settle Barry down enough to have dinner with Casey and him in hopes of getting Casey and Barry together, or at least having Casey be able to find out from Barry what her plans would be and how she would get out of the Dominican Republic, and when. And, of course, there was no pinning Barry down about returning home with her. This thought left a bottomless pit in her stomach, because what was happening to her at Casa del Campo was so unreal that she had to start thinking about what Chicago was going to be like when she returned.

Barry had started growing a beard and really thought he was Jesus Christ superstar. He was a Jesus freak. This was the start of his fantasies relating to music and song lyrics. Barry was living from the lyrics of the songs of the early seventies. Casey could even tell what he was going to do by the albums that he was listening to. It was bizarre.

It didn't take Casey long to figure out that these were his motivations and that if she wanted to relate to him, it would have to be in this way. She could also recognize that some of his moves and some of his decisions were made for him through the lyrics of songs that he liked, or would listen to. Casey didn't want to believe that this was really happening to her, but it was, and she had no control over the situation. She just wanted to get home to the children. She really hadn't totally gotten her strength back from Leslye's birth, and she felt very tired and rundown, but exhilarated at the same time. She looked beautiful and radiant.

Barry would talk to Casey for short periods of time and their communication was great. It was even a sexual turn on for Casey and this was not a normal feeling. And then something would set him off and that was it. Off he would go and disappear for a few days, and Casey would wait to make her next contact. Meanwhile, she had notified Florence and Max to let them know that something was wrong, but there was very little communication back. So she was basically on her own.

It was a scary experience. Casey knew that Barry was planning on leaving soon and she had to make sure that he had her booked out on a flight home. She could not be sure at this point where he was going to be going from here. She could not be sure at this point as to how broken down his mind was. There was such a thin line between behavioral patterns that determined a normal mind and a sick one.

Casey was exhausted and really wanted to get the hell out of this horror. She was beside herself and decided that she had to get out of this place even if it meant leaving Barry and his craziness, but she wanted to get home to John and Lesley. Casey missed the kids so. She was able to determine from the airlines that her tickets were not cancelled, so she made the decision to take the reservation and think about departing, which would give her a day and a half to pack, find Barry and tell him, and hopefully get him to respond to this idea. And also, to try to find where he may be going.

Mark was able to find out that Barry was going to go to Marrakech with Lisa Minelli's band who traveled everywhere with her and who were there because she was performing at the hotel. The reason for this trip was to pick up hashish in Marrakech. Casey was able to find this out by getting high with the band at the pool all morning. She was so relaxed and this was great. She needed to be because she had to convince Barry to have brunch with her and figure out her plan for checking out of the hotel.

He really roared when she said to him, "Can you imagine the look on your parents' faces when I get off the plane without you? And tell them that you are in Marrakech." She was using this as an element of shock, hoping he might return to reality, but actually, he was most amused by the whole thing.

Casey and Barry said their farewells and it was quite loving. Casey was so confused. She just decided to relax and let it happen. She did know that Max and Florence would be there to meet her when she arrived in Chicago. This would be her sobering factor, but she was not going to deal with that until she got off the plane.

She had heard rumors that Barry was fucking his brains off and she was kind of turned on because she had never imagined him as being so desirous. You would think this would disturb her, but it really didn't. She was probably numb anyway. The only thing that Casey could flash through her mind was the children and would this have happened if her father were alive. At least he would be here to help. The only person she could rely on for help would be Mark and her attorney, Kevin. Mark would get her out of this country. Barry in Marrakech and hashish?

Casey checked out of the hotel. She looked suntanned, well dressed and beautiful, and Mark was nice enough to take her to the airport with a driver. She felt good because she had smoked a joint with the band just before she left, hoping to pick up anything else she could on Barry and his plan, but all she learned was what a bitch Lisa Minelli was. By now Casey knew she wasn't the crazy one because they had all confessed to her that he was definitely ill and needed help. They didn't want to be responsible for him but there was no way that Barry was going to change his plans. So he was on his own from here. Casey knew that her responsibilities were at home.

The first part of the trip to Miami was all right. The thought kept rushing through Casey's mind about what she was going to say to the Brickmans. She did know that she was not going to be intimidated by them and she just remembered that she would use her dad's forceful, easy and trustful manner to get her through this situation. After all, she didn't have the nervous breakdown, and she was not going to take any abuse from these schmucks.

The plane change in Miami was relatively simple. The only thing that Casey had to deal with was that because she was so young, she was paranoid about all of the people on the plane that she knew and what to say if anyone asked where Barry was. Every familiar eye was on her in the plane. Luckily, it was filled and she was sitting next to a stranger in the rear. She knew if asked she would say Barry was bumped from the plane and she had to take her reservation, and that he was on stand-by. It was so weird not having Barry with her. She was so vulnerable to many opportunities and was especially careful because of that. Casey was aware of her beauty and was always careful to set people around her at ease because of it. Casey felt a surge of power and she liked the independence that she was experiencing. It was exciting and she was very motivated by the excitement.

9

The plane was approaching O'Hare and the fasten seat belts sign was on. Casey was tired and anxious to go home and hug the children. Florence and Max were there to meet her and all that she wanted to do was get away from the crowds at the airport before she broke down herself. The usual disembarking and collecting of the luggage and getting organized and to the car took a few moments, and then they were away from the crowds and able to talk in the car.

Casey told them what she had briefly told them on the phone -- that Barry was acting strange and she thought he was having a nervous breakdown. She told how bizarre he had been on the trip and that she wasn't sure but thought he was on his way to Morocco and that they were going to Marrakech. She said she wasn't sure that he might not be in some danger because he had made friends with a weird group and it was beyond her control and very frustrating, especially because the communication was so bad.

Max joked a bit and he seemed rather concerned and concerned for the children, but it was hard to tell what he was thinking. She told them that Barry had the check book and that she didn't even have money for groceries. He always liked to play the big man, so he had kissed her when he left the house and slipped her a couple of hundred dollars. She needed this because Daddy wasn't around to depend on. Casey was exhausted and left her unpacking and went and woke the children up, hugged and kissed them, and played with them a while.

Casey's next thought as she was getting ready for bed was to call Kevin Daniels, her attorney, who was a friend of the family, and tell him of this whole bizarre episode. She needed a father image and knew it couldn't be Max. She also needed an attorney and confidante. Kevin was ready for action. He was also very supportive and funny. After all, only a good sense of humor could have gotten Casey through some of the trauma she had to deal with.

She proceeded to tell Kevin the whole story of Barry's change in personality and, of course, that he was on his way to Marrakech and could be in dangerous company.

Barry's perspectives were totally off and his judgments were poor, making him very vulnerable while traveling in the situation that he was in. It was a miracle that he wasn't robbed or accosted during his travels, especially with his mind in a deformed state. This was a mess and you can't think about what you don't have, but Casey sure would like her daddy now.

Barry had arrived in Morocco, which could almost be compared to a third world country, the ambiance being quite different than Europe or any form of civilization. The streets of Marrakech were packed with people and the smell of hashish was everywhere. There were animals in the streets -- camels and donkeys. It kind of created a mystique about the place.

Barry was just high and the group that he travelled with were high on hashish. Barry's function in the group was going to be to carry the hashish out of the country. As he was the innocent bystander and totally oblivious to what was happening, he would have no guilt to even carry with him, nor would they have to pay someone to do the job. So it was a beneficial position all the way around. However, Barry was really being taken such advantage of.

The connection was made and Barry was taken to a party in one of Marrakech's finest areas. He was given a robe and sandals to wear. He met some interesting people and really started to enjoy native Moroccan style when suddenly he became very dizzy. He had been given a sedative and his head was laid back on a pillow. This was done, watched and executed very meticulously because it was important that Barry not be injured or hurt, and the hashish planted on him unknowingly so that he could get it out of the country for them.

The party was winding down and Barry was coming to. He was told that he passed out cold and was fine. Then he was transferred back to the hotel in a limousine, unaware that the shipment of dope had been sewn into his pants. He didn't spend a moment away from one of the band members. Barry's naiveté, of course, was interpreted with no ulterior motives and he was quite pleased with the attention and being sought after so aggressively. His every move was closely watched.

He got through Customs all right and again was rushed off in a limousine to an old garage in Brooklyn. Everything had gone pretty smoothly until now, when he was hit over the head. He started hyperventilating and his eyes started to roll, but he did not pass out. In a panic, his pants holding the shipment of dope were removed and he was left there to lie. These were all things that Casey never found out about until after Barry was committed to Gracie Square Hospital. It was that or Bellevue where he would have had derelict treatment. What a nightmare this had all been.

Somehow Barry made it into Manhattan and he was found walking out of St. Paul's Cathedral. The police believed him when he said that he was held up and they drove him to the Regency, where he said his luggage was sent from the airport. He was able to stay there because it was late and the manager knew him from previous visits.

The hotel was concerned and thought that a family member should be notified.

It was Monday morning when Casey got the call of this horrifying event. She notified Kevin and Max and Florence and before unpacking her resort suitcase, she was on her way to New York. They arrived at the Regency and learned more details of what had been going on. Kevin arrived shortly after and Casey cried when she saw him, she was so pleased to have some support. It was getting very oppressive, just being with Max and Florence. It was suggested that Barry be examined and also a psychiatrist was called in on the case.

When Casey thought about what had happened and all of the events that had taken place, she felt a tinge of excitement. There was nothing normal or mundane about what she was going through and she certainly became aware that she was motivated by action. She loved excitement.

Things were settling down a little and there was not a lot to be said about Florence and Max's company. Casey thought she might lose her mind if she continued to spend too much time with these people. Breakfast, lunch and dinner were just too much.

At this point no decisions had been made regarding Barry. He was quite ill and not functioning very well on his own. A doctor was called in and tried to talk to Barry. At this point it was next to impossible. His power of concentration was limited and he could barely carry on any kind of conversation for more than a few minutes at a time. Most of it focused around persecution and great splits in personality. He constantly jumped from one subject to the next, showing all emotions of love, hate and anger. Casey almost lost her composure when Barry told his father that he should learn to relax and enjoy life a little. They were too domineering as parents, and he compared his dad to Portnoy in Roth's book that was quite popular at the time. He continued with the nervous stomach syndrome that Portnoy's father had, pains in his chest, and similar bathroom habits, and said that he didn't want to end up like that.

Barry's expressions and looks were priceless, as well as the shock of truth on the faces of his parents. Casey only kept saying to herself at the time, I'm not really here listening to all this, because they will never forgive me for being witness to all this. If nothing else, it was like taking a crash course in psychology and what not to do with your children when they are growing up. And it was hard to hold back her laughter.

Kevin missed all of this but Casey filled him in over a glass of champagne in the bar at the Regency. It was a relief not to have Florence and Max around. Kevin's description of them was nondescript and quite funny, as was the way he referred to Max as helpful and supportive felons. We were definitely speaking the same language.

Kevin continued to tell her how crazy Barry was and that Gracie Square, a private hospital that he had been committed to, could not make any promises as to the length of time that his recovery would take. He was totally out of touch with reality. Casey was seeing Dr. Kaplan but she was unable to see Barry. Kevin remarked that it was better that she not see him in this condition. Some of the events that took place were concluded with a touch of humor. It was the only way to get through this crisis, sick as it might sound.

Casey started to tell Kevin that Barry imagined her as a very sensuous and sought-after woman, and he had fantasies of affairs with many men who were in her life. Casey could not imagine where he got these feelings. However, Dr. Kaplan told her this was a very common occurrence in a total nervous breakdown. He felt insufficient, not capable of fulfillment as a man, wanting to break away from his father's identity. It was also a great boost to his ego to imagine a woman who he has possessed sexually was highly desirable to other men and many other men.

The whole fantasy sickened Casey. Although she did tell Kevin that she knew that she was desirous but that another man's attention did make her feel a little guilty because she was sensitive enough to know that it could have an effect on Barry.

It really wasn't until Casey had solidified her relationship with Randy, and infidelity was a subject which they discussed very openly in their relationship, that she could really cope with and be relaxed talking to another man at a party and know that she would not be paranoid about his wife's reaction, or worry that he would verbally seduce her in the first few minutes of their conversation. If he was doing this, she knew how to handle it and she was a lady.

She became much more confident of herself and mature and she could handle a situation like this quite well. Randy and she could discuss extramarital sex quite openly and they knew that they were in total agreement with each other, and they could keep their communication lines open. Being able to discuss very private subjects such as these kept their relationship closer than ever and they were very sexually compatible.

Barry was having fantasies about Casey and saying how he caught her in bed with her decorator and that she was having an affair with their neighbor and his best friend. And even with her gynecologist. Can one imagine Dr. Morton, who delivered John and Lesley? It was more absurd than anything she had had to deal with. Casey learned a lot and fast and Dr. Kaplan gave her so much confidence and support, and Casey was well aware that she was not only smart but sensitive

He also thought that he was a persecuted person and unloved and very much deserted by everyone. Casey was so upset by all the events that were occurring and she suddenly felt sick, nauseous, and very lonely. She wanted to help Barry so, to hold him, love him, and it seemed to unfair that he was the most unresponsive to her, especially when she knew that he loved her the most. Nothing was normal, nothing was in its proper perspective. It kind of made her appreciate normal things and made her wonder about life. Casey realized that she was going to be living on the edge. She also knew that she was going to have to prove herself as a person and knew that she must depend on herself for her own survival and that of Lesley and John.

Barry was still restless and very hyper, and the decision was suggested by the doctor called in that he should be committed to a hospital. However, he could not be committed by his wife in case he carried any resentment with it. Kevin had arranged everything and also arranged for Max to commit him. Casey unwittingly found all this out later. Casey couldn't see him at all during this time, but she decided that her place was in New York with him.

She continued to stay on at the Regency for a few days, hoping to learn something of Barry's condition. She had to spend a great deal of time with Max and Florence, which was boring and devastating.

There were even times when Casey felt they needed help worse than Barry. Kevin told Casey that Max was worried that she would spend too much money while they were in New York. Can you imagine? Casey was devastated when she heard this and had all that she could do to pull herself together, get a manicure, and have her hair conditioned, since she hadn't had a chance to do this when she returned home. She was also finding that room service was more enjoyable than dining with Barry's parents, the Brickmans.

Casey could see that they were all going to be spending some time in New York during this waiting period to try to establish Barry's condition, and what the next step to be taken would be. She also knew that she would be smart to call some friends who lived in the city and tell them of her problems. Folly was on call and by her side. She even came and stayed with her at the hotel after Florence and Max left.

Folly was able to go and visit with Barry, telling Casey that he was really gone. Casey called Leonard and Sandy Roberts, whom they had met while traveling in the South of France, and Richard Gordon, who was a good friend that they had met in Paradise Island and also was in the South of France with all of them. It was a relief to get together with these people even if she had to subject them to Florence and Max.

Leonard charmed the pants off of Max, sent flowers to their suite and took them all to dinner. Casey did not realize that Leonard, who was a very sophisticated businessman and investment banker of well means, asked Max to loan him $15,000. This was not so bad, but the sad thing to Casey was that Max, who was the cheapest bastard, was totally taken in by Leonard's charm. Max lent him the money, of course, never to see it again.

When Barry heard this story he was quite upset because to think that he would never do something like this, a favor, for his own son, and he accommodated a perfect stranger without even checking a reference or even discussing it with Casey, who would have advised him not to get involved, and that it wasn't important to

Barry. The whole incident was terribly disturbing to Casey, to think that Max would act on such instinctive stupidity and especially at a time like this.

Casey was becoming concerned about the progress of Barry's condition. She was frustrated because there was nothing that she could do about it. Florence and Max had decided to go home but Casey did not feel comfortable about leaving yet. She felt that by being in New York and in touch with Barry's doctor and available to see Barry, that she was more in touch with Barry. It was so frustrating because she didn't know what to do. She wanted to be with the children, but thought she belonged with Barry.

Florence and Max went back to Chicago but Casey spent a few more days in New York. When the doctor told her it was all right to leave, she went home to the children. She was home three days when she was called back to New York because Barry wanted to see her. He was now very passive which was a result of the medication. It was as if his personality had transversed into another person. He was different. It was scary, but Casey managed to act quite normal and composed.

After leaving the hospital, she was so sick to her stomach that she could hardly hold her head up. She got back to the hotel and rested before dinner.

10

Folly called Casey and she talked about Barry. Folly had seen him just after Casey left. It was a most depressing subject. Folly couldn't believe how weird the whole thing was. Casey asked if she wanted to have dinner, but she couldn't because she had to attend a meeting and dinner with her husband. Casey was taken to L'Grennoille for dinner by Leonard and Sandy.

That evening she became violently ill and called Folly. Folly came to be with her and took her to Dr. Claps in the morning. It was 'nerves,' and Casey decided to go back to Chicago.

It was good to be back home with the children and try to get some semblance of normality. Casey finally was feeling stronger and went to see her mother who knew her but who could not remember anything that Casey was telling her about Barry or what was happening around her. Casey could see she was hopeless and just made sure that she was comfortable, presentable and that her house was being maintained properly. This was not easy, but Casey managed to keep all things in order. She had two in help taking care of Margaret and running the house in addition to Ed, who had been the houseman when Casey was in high school and Aunt Rae, who thrived on the need to help others. It was good companionship for Mother, and good therapy for Aunt Rae.

Much time had elapsed and John and Lesley were growing quite beautiful. They had gotten through their terrible twos and John was finishing nursery school, getting ready to start kindergarten. And Lesley was still in nursery school, smart, alert, and just beautiful. Barry was enjoying the children in spite of his illness and his problems coping, and Casey cherished them, loved them, and only wished that life would look more optimistic with Barry. She felt as if she were living on the edge of a cliff, and the excitement was overwhelming. She at times wished that her life was mundane and boring.

Barry had been traveling with Casey, as he depended greatly on her. They traveled to Europe, New York, and California, and Barry wanted to leave his family business, even though Max didn't know, and buy a rock group. This was cultivated in the hospital when he entered it in Chicago, and met and made a very close friend with the person who was going to be the booking agent. They were going to make a lot of money and this is what Barry wanted to do.

Casey knew herself that she didn't want this, but she went along with Barry for his own mental well being. Casey was very torn, but she had to think of herself and the children. Casey and Barry met Elton John and the Beach Boys and there was a lot of excitement in their lives. They were exposed to drugs and a whole new attitude about life. It was quite different from the regimen they had practiced at home. It was very unrealistic.

Margaret's heart was failing and when Casey was called about her death, she felt numb. She knew it was coming, but indeed, it was a big loss and a great shock.

Casey had made many visits to see Barry at the hospital and with each breakdown, she hoped it would be the last. But in reality, she was beginning to face the fact that this was a chronic condition, and even when he returned home the very last time before his death, drained mentally and physically, but somehow she always managed to look just beautiful, she wanted to believe that everything was going to be all right. He really was great over the weekend when Douglas and Jennifer stopped over and he looked great too. Margaret's untimely death and Barry's illness were starting to take a toll on Casey. She was busy with the children especially because John had just started kindergarden and she was anxious to spend as much time as possible with him. Barry went to work as usual that week.

It was Tuesday and Barry got up and got dressed for the office. The children were up and Casey was busy with them. Emma was making breakfast and everything seemed fine. They all had breakfast together. Casey walked John up the driveway to the bus and Lesley was picked up for nursery school. Casey was not going to her painting class today because she had to shop for groceries since she and Barry were going to New York on Wednesday and Barry had even consented to see Folly's psychiatrist while they were there. Barry was already seeing a different doctor in Chicago and they thought it would be a good idea for somebody else's opinion on the case.

Casey saw the children off and then Barry drove off in his own Porsche. It was a relatively normal day. Emma was cleaning up the breakfast dishes and Casey and she loaded the Mercedes with the geranium plants from the patio. She was going to take them to the cemetery for her parents and then go see Aunt Rae and visit with her and tell her to have a nice holiday. It was Rosh Hashanah, the Jewish New Year.

Casey talked to Folly briefly. Everything was all set and Folly, who had just separated from Howard, was expecting them. Casey was doing her errands on her way to the cemetery when she suddenly thought of Folly fucking. In fact, that was all that she could think about as she drove. She could see Folly's wet kisses all over Adam's body and Adam caressing and kissing Folly all over. His tongue was slowly exploring every crack and crevice. His lips found that special spot between her legs and she could hear Folly's moans of pleasure as she came in his mouth. Casey came at this moment as she was driving. She was so wet. The intensity was terribly exciting to Casey. She approached the cemetery in a cold sweat, but quickly pulled herself together. This trip was dull and depressing, but dutiful.

As Casey arrived at Aunt Rae's for a short visit, she thought she should check in with Emma. Emma was mumbling, something was wrong. She said the children weren't home from school and Dr. Switzer had called and said that Casey should meet him at Barry's parents. Casey asked Emma why there, and she didn't know, but that was the message.

Casey felt numb. She didn't know what to think. She couldn't speak. But she left Aunt Rae calmly so she would not alarm her, but she said something was wrong. In Casey's numbness she also felt a surge of excitement and a feeling of relief, but she wasn't sure why, nor could she call Dr. Switzer.

Casey approached the Brickmans. There were a lot of cars at the house. She pulled in the driveway and was met by Dr. Switzer who told her that Barry left his office with no explanation or note and drove to a building where the Ritz Carleton is, where he may have been visiting someone, but no one seems to know. He apparently jumped from the top of the building, leaving his Porsche parked at the building perfectly intact and untouched. He was crushed beyond recognition. Some sunbathers at the pool reported the incident to the police, as well as an elderly lady who was entering the back of the building at the moment his body hit the ground. Murder was immediately ruled out. In his wallet the police found Dr. Switzer's number and called him for the identification. The body was at the morgue and had to be moved immediately.

Casey was absolutely stunned. However, she knew that she would need all of the strength God had to give her to get through this ordeal. Casey collapsed in Dr. Switzer's arms. He held her and was able to get her into the house. Casey was uncontrollable. She was given a sedative and she knew she must get to the children. Dr. Switzer thought it best that since they were so young, to let them continue the day normally and be put to bed and be told about their father early the next morning. He would come to the house and Casey and he would tell the children at breakfast.

Casey called Emma who asked if Mr. "B" was all right. Casey said no, she couldn't talk, she would explain when she got home, just that she was unable to talk, and to please take care of John and Lesley and she would be home as soon as possible, and to please take care, and that if anyone called, that she was at the Brickmans and she would talk to her later.

Everybody was sedated and shocked. Dr. Switzer was great support to Casey. Casey was devastated, but she also had a great deal of strength.

Folly had been notified and had already made reservations to come to Chicago to be with Casey. They spoke briefly. Casey felt comfort and relief, knowing that Folly was going to come and spend time with her. Casey was absolutely exhausted and really wanted to be home with the children, but she had to take care of some last minute details before she left Barry's parents.

They had decided to have the funeral immediately due to the fact that a holiday was the next day, and if they didn't, they would have to wait until after the holiday. This didn't seem appropriate. The news spread fast and although the announcement in the paper was small, the funeral was huge.

Casey had managed to get some sleep, which she badly needed, and to be up at sunrise, because before the funeral she had to meet with Dr. Switzer at her house and tell the children what had happened, and take care of the usual legalities that one takes care of at this time.

Kevin and Dr. Switzer got her through the morning along with the support of her friends who were wonderful. Casey had so many things to deal with and she was not dealing with herself yet or the shock. She was doing what she had to do.

Young children are so resilient, but Casey knew that she had a lot ahead of her in dealing with the children. Casey had hardly gotten over the death of her parents, and now she had such grief over Barry.

Casey hoped that she would get through the next twenty-four hours. The decision had been made to have the children remain at home with Emma, that it would be better for them. Casey would need all the support that she could get as she had no family to rely on. Folly was at her side and she would be greatly relieved to have the funeral pass and get through this ordeal.

11

The funeral was huge. Barry would have been pleased to know that it was comparable in size to Ralph's when he died. Casey really didn't know that Barry had so many friends. She had been given something to help her relax and she needed it because she knew that all eyes were on her. The limousines drove up and Casey became very weak, so weak that she lost all of her strength and she couldn't move. Folly gave her smelling salts. She didn't look like she was going to faint, but she couldn't get out of the car.

With the help of the Rabbi and Folly, she got out of the car and staggered to a chair that was waiting for her so that the service could proceed.

Casey was wearing her dark glasses and she was quite aware of who was in attendance at this funeral. It was overwhelming. She was only feeling a numbness and actually acting very much in control for someone so drugged.

There were bankers, hippies, politicians, movie and video people, friends, and a lot of acquaintances. Barry loved life. He was so sick, but nobody knew how sick he really was. He lived big, he did a lot. His death was a monumental statement.

She thought, he didn't seem to want to hurt anyone, but he certainly did hurt himself, because we are all here to survive. And he's not. Nobody can judge, the only thing to do is to do what you have to do and take care of the things most important, and go on with a new life. Casey knew this, and this is what she did. She really knew what she wanted and what was the best for John and Leslye.

Casey felt numbness and felt so bad that Barry was this ill and she didn't know it. At the same time, she felt relief, which she also felt guilty about. She was angry about the whole thing, which is natural, but as she was told by Dr. Switzer, that feeling would pass. It did pass, and soon. The feeling of relief was the best feeling that she had and this gave her the strength and hope that she needed to go on and to deal with the children, because this was her problem and she knew that she couldn't depend on Florence and Max for any kind of support.

Lauren was Casey's strength during and after the funeral. She knew just who Casey was comfortable with and shifted people around the house after the memorial service. She was able to tell when Casey was disturbed and was able to help and save her from a great deal of trauma.

Casey knew that if she had her strength she would get through anything. She slowly started to regain her strength and energy and deal with all of the details following Barry's death as well as spending a lot of time with Leslye and John. She was slowly starting to think of a new life as she got all of her financial matters taken care of. Everything was starting to fall into the right perspective. She was very lucky that money was not a problem for her at this time. Casey felt relief and strength and a tremendous zest for life. Being an Aquarius gave Casey strength, common sense, the ability to judge a situation and power to make it happen. Casey, who listened to her body, was able to stay in control and move spiritually, and emotionally, and take care of most situations that she was confronted with. She discovered that most always she picked the best and most rational way to handle any problems that occurred. Casey also thought the less said the better, as she was high profile, coping by acting low profile, and she was well aware that her answers were the best for the children, and herself and anything that meant moving forward in this very complicated life.

Friends meant well and everyone had their two cents to add, and Casey could handle that and not become self destructive or influenced by everyone's advice, she knew what was best for John, Lesley, and herself.

As casey got older she grew more beautiful and intelligent, and was most desirable, a real sweetheart. She knew how to handle herself, minipulate herself and others, and be very smooth at it.

12

Randy was getting bored with all of the women who wanted to take care of him and run his life, and even the gorgeous young things that he was playing around with were not enough fulfillment for him and one thing he was not, was dumb.

His business was going well and of course this gave him the opportunity to pretty much be able to have the flexibility that he wanted with his personal life. Harry would drool when Randy would relate the experiences of being single again but all of the fantasies were great for fleeting moments; however, Randy knew that he had to develop some stability to his life eventually. The perimeters of dating and single life were different and much more liberal because this was before any knowledge of AIDS or the danger of it.

Life had been very hectic for Casey since Barry committed suicide. She had to regain her strength and energy, and deal with the children herself.

She was receiving friends from all over the world and everyone wanted to help her with her grief and make her feel better. She was invited everywhere and to the best parties. She was thrown in with the very heights of society, the horse and country set, and she was entertained by some of Barry's musician and rock band friends, whom he originally made contacts with in the hospital when he had his breakdown. She was seeing life at its fullest and from all angles.

Casey enjoyed a puff on a joint from time to time, it was very relaxing and she did come in contact with drugs, but it was social and not habit forming. Casey had only fantasized about being involved in an orgy or a "ménage a trois" but suddenly her life was taking an interesting turn. She was still able to manage to run a perfect home and keep stability around the children, and also find out that she was living most of her fantasies. Soon she found out that she was everybody's darling, adored by all, young, beautiful, a wealthy widow. Casey was more in control of her own life then she had ever been, and so young, beautiful and desirable.

That, alone, was a fantasy. She was very cautious about how to act and how to treat those that could cause her problems. Casey knew that her presence was sometimes intimidating and it was important that she make friends and acquaintances feel comfortable around her. She was a pro at this, a manipulator.

Randy felt a tinge of excitement when he thought of meeting her, a young widow, how helpless Casey must be. He knew that he should wait to meet her but his anxieties overwhelmed him and he called her as soon as Harry gave him the information about her horse that was for sale. What a ploy -- Randy was absolutely turned on and was starting to anticipate how he was going to get past the first phone call without an erection.

Randy was overwhelmed by the sexual proclivities that he was encountering while going through his divorce. He had married at age 22 and he had a multitude of suppressed fantasies that were being uncorked now.

He hadn't met a nice girl since he had been separated. They were either after him for his money and position, or so young and far out that this was not what he felt secure with. He sure was having a good time and the women loved him. Randy couldn't wait to meet Casey, maybe because she was different, she wasn't divorced. He knew he wanted to sleep with her but he was contemplating how and when and this was exciting. His sympathies went out to her because she was young and beautiful, alone and, he thought, helpless. Little did he know.

Casey was having a hard time finding hours in the day for herself; she was so busy and certainly being taken care of. It was not hard for Casey to act and be proper, it was inbred in her. This was her rebellion, her immaturity. She, of course, acted so extremely proper. If she took advantage of every offer that she had she would be mentally and physically exhausted. Her friends fantasized about her but she was very careful and very particular and she had an impeccable reputation and was respected by everyone, including her peers. She was smart. She was private.

Casey was invited to orgies by friends that she not only thought were straight but square as well, but she really wasn't ready for this, nor did she need to express herself sexually, nor was she ready for this now. Her painting was quite enough self-expression for her at this time, after what she had been through with Barry's death. She did go to an orgy with Craig and Madeline Clark and just observed the whole thing. Casey knew immediately this scene was not for her. Not in Chicago, not in 1972, not in 2012. Maybe in the South of France, but nowhere and now, and really never, with the discovery of the AIDS virus. Craig was madly in love and smitten with Casey's beauty, and he knew that he had to have her. Although she did not find him physically attractive, she thought he was interesting to talk to, very intellectual, a good listener, but no wit or sense of humor. The more she could talk to him and be with him intellectually, the more she could get interested in him physically.

Peter called her many times, which she thought was a nice gesture out of friendship and respect to her parents, Margaret and Ralph. This attraction went back to childhood even though Casey was considerably younger than Peter Munson. He invited her to his country estate and they had a delicious lunch, fine champagne, "Dom," and talked most of the afternoon. The attraction was overwhelming. When they kissed it was more than just friendship, and Casey wasn't afraid to let one thing lead to another even though Peter was divorced. She knew this was not for her but she felt safe and secure and it felt good. The servants were gone and only the caretaker was working around the formal gardens. Casey and Peter kissed and just lounged on the patio in the sun. Their bodies were both feeling the same kind of heat and throbbing synergy, and this time when Casey kissed Peter she knew this wasn't going to be the last time. The scene of them fucking in the gardens of his parents' home before Barry and she got married kept flashing through her mind. Peter had always loved Casey and lusted for her beauty. He also knew in his own mind that he wasn't enough for her.

Dr. Bond had told Casey, when Barry was in the hospital, that a young woman in her position needs a sexual outlet as well as a physical one, and that this would be good for her. Casey was shocked and didn't agree with him but this was the guilt from her parents and her upbringing that was haunting her.

This assignation with Peter for Casey was a safe thing and really done as a necessity for a physical and sexual longing that she needed. It was safe and had no emotional involvement and she felt good, looked great, and her therapist said it was good for her.

Casey had such a soft perfect baby face and Peter loved this because it also made him feel so good. She also had the softest skin and the most beautiful full breasts that he had ever seen. Her nipples were always erect and his cock was also erect, holding back with a great deal of control. She was ready and wet and always so receptive.

Peter always expressed how much alike they were. Casey could never completely share these feelings and especially after she had been introduced to Randy Edwards, fourth generation Mainline and so divinely handsome.

Thoughts of Peter faded very fast, all that Casey could think about was Randy. She loved him, she was overwhelmed by his attention. What a man. She forgot about every other man in her life because Randy seemed to satisfy and fufill all her needs. She was happy, content, and so in love. She wasn't afraid, she saw a secure future for the children and for herself.

Randy had suggested that Casey come to Europe with him. She was elated by the invitation. Think of how she felt when she saw Peter on the Orient Express when she was with Randy. There was no feeling, she didn't even want to be noticed by him. To think that she could have fucked up her life with him. Randy knew about him, and although her relationship with Peter was understandable and did go back to her childhood, Randy was extremely jealous. He supported her and believed her and knew that no matter what, it was over.

Peter and Casey would never be together, he was too dysfunctional. He was so in love with her, he felt that Casey broke up his marriage, and he also had a revenge to break up her marriage with Randy and to cause any kind of trouble that he could. Randy loathed him and was shattered by him.

13

Reality was always hard to come back to, but Casey always managed to snap back fast, probably because she went through Barry's illness with him and never wanted to see herself like that. It Seemed Barry's death brought her strength.

She had arrived home after lunch and dinner with Peter and was totally relaxed. Reality was always a sobering effect on Casey and it never took her long to move into action and function as she had to. John and Leslye would be coming home soon and she was so excited to see them! In the midst of all this a call came from Randy. Randy Edwards. Casey's heart started to undulate.

Through this very polite conversation Casey could also see a future for John, Lesley and herself. She was not going to fuck up if there was anything to this. She and Randy talked about all the right things and immediately established a rapport with each other. The only thing that scared her was the thought that kept crossing her mind that he must treat all women this way, or was it that she was special? It was marvelous. He was so charming. Life was scary but so exciting, and Casey loved excitement.

Casey was scared and intimidated. Randy was a very powerful person with a lot of connections and as madly in love with him as she was, she could not help but be overwhelmed by his prestige, power and wealth.

Casey was independently wealthy herself and she didn't want to be intimidated or belittled by anyone else's money or power, but a man of lesser status than her would not be challenging enough to her. She also didn't want to lose her own identity and at times it was difficult.

14

Casey always disliked the envy that Peter had created between his first wife Laurel and herself. She resented being put in a situation like that and that was probably one reason she didn't trust Peter. Laurel Munson, now Laurel Benson, always wanted what Casey had and they couldn't be friends because there was too much competition between them and Laurel couldn't be trusted. She was very nice and charming on the surface, but a very self-centered and relentless bitch.

When Casey returned from the Dominican Republic and Barry was so ill, Laurel was burning with jealousy because she was home with her children and Casey was moving fast, traveling back and forth to New York. Casey hadn't mentioned the breakdown but Laurel knew something was happening and began to spread horrible rumors about the Brickman's and about Casey. Casey terminated their friendship but Peter tried to keep it going. Their relationship was never good from that point on.

Peter never stopped desiring Casey but it was impossible for them to be friends. Casey had no love for Peter either, she thought he was crude and always blamed him for the animosity that was caused between Laurel and herself. Peter could be a toy in her life but Casey needed a real man to satisfy her.

Casey felt bad when she heard that Peter and Laurel were having problems, but she had no desire to get involved. She would never be a friend to Laurel Munson, however she always liked Peter but not enough. They could be good friends.

Peter kept coming into Casey's life. Sometimes it was comforting.

Peter was tormenting and annoying to Casey until she met Randy. She didn't want to see him, she didn't want him in her life, but he always seemed to be there. Seeing Peter on the Orient Express was kind of exciting and that was such a change in Casey's emotions because if she hadn't been with Randy, she would have felt much more discomfort.

Folly loved to fuck, or if she didn't, she tried to fuck every man that she came in contact with. Peter and Randy were no exceptions. She and Casey had an interesting relationship and Casey and she shared and lent their men a lot. This made them even closer.

Folly was a tough woman and Casey learned a lot from her, but Casey was able to use Folly's positive and aggressiveness to her advantage and still maintain her femininity and be successful with what she wanted to accomplish. Folly wasn't always; however Casey had more going for her and was able to use what she learned to its advantage. Folly also learned from Casey and followed her advice, but Casey was able to accomplish more for herself.

Margaret and Ralph died when Casey was still very young and naive. Casey had no family support or help from her parents for stroking, and this was hard. She needed this from Randy and at this point in their love and relationship, she didn't know that this would be a problem. She was able to get this support from her brother-in-law who also had the same problem dealing with Randy. Unfortunately, Randy had to tear down everyone's self-esteem around in order to build up his own and feel secure. This would be his downfall. It was a very devious method of retaining power and control and he would live to regret that he treated people this way and thought he could get away with it.

Casey differed. Casey <u>was</u> <u>not</u> a self-destructive person. Casey could determine her goals and take care of herself.

One goal that was important to Casey was to get John and Leslye and herself out of limbo and create a solid family unit for them. She knew that Peter Munson would be a waste of time for her and that he did not offer her what she needed for self-fulfillment.

15

Randy and Casey had many phone conversations before they met. Randy was anxious to meet Casey but Casey wanted to be sure that when she did meet him she was ready, and still needed some time for Randy Edwards. Casey finally consented to have Randy come to her house for a drink. She did not feel comfortable going anywhere public with him yet, it was too early. She did want to meet him. She was dying with curious anticipation.

Folly never left Casey for the first few months after Barry died. She came to Chicago from New York to be with her and they took John and Leslye to Florida, and she really helped Casey through this difficult period. It was also helping Folly because she was coming out of one of the worst periods that had affected her from her divorce. Casey and Folly could talk and they were relaxed when they were together and they had never both been unmarried at the same time since they knew each other, (change Folly's name)

(except for camp. This was great therapy for both of them, and you can be sure that if there wasn't something in it for Folly, she wouldn't have done it.

They had some interesting sexual experiences together. They became very close friends and replaced for each other a good sister relationship. They could be totally honest with each other and that was great. Folly seemed to have a love and admiration for Casey and Casey admired Folly's independence and strength, even though she always said that Casey was stronger.

Having mixed emotions about meeting Randy at this time and maybe it had something to do with the fear of rejection and the anticipation being over, Casey weakened in her last conversation with Randy. (Folly) Peggy and she both listened as he spoke and they figured that they must meet this man now and Casey wanted to get a look at him while she was in town. Casey told Randy that she would love to meet him and that her friend was in from New York. She asked if he would come for a drink on Sunday and she really did not want to let on how excited she was to meet him.

It was Thanksgiving, and holidays were always depressing, even though they all went to the Clarks for dinner. Both Peggy and Casey did what they wanted to do, if they didn't want to stay at dinner, they would leave. There was no such thing as being polite, you had to do what you felt. Madeline sometimes got jealous of Peggy and Casey, so they were careful not to offend her since she was being so nice to them. It occurred to Casey that Clark was lusting for both Peggy and herself and probably Madeline too, but it was definitely out of the question at this time. They also got similar feelings from Madeline, but they were only there to have dinner and they were looking forward to meeting Randy and maybe even one of his friends for Folly. The rest of the weekend consisted of a few more dinners and constructive time that Casey and Folly spent with the children.

Douglas took them all to a movie one night and out to eat. On Sunday, Randy had called and he stopped over for a drink with Jack Lang. This was the first time Casey had met him, and there was an immediate attraction between Randy and Casey. The children met these two men and their reaction was incredible. They went wild, they were showing off, laughing, running around screaming, actually acting obnoxious, but if Randy and Jack stopped to analyze why they reacted this way, they would have been very flattered. John was especially excited. Because this was the first male that he had met that to him seemed like he could be a father to him and therefore the anxiety and enthusiasm was overwhelming.

Casey was mortified and she did not know what to do nor did she know how to react. Peggy tried to settle the children down by taking them upstairs and bribing them. Randy's first feeling for Casey was sympathy and compassion and wanting to help this poor girl. Jack thought the children were obnoxious, but later learned differently.

The meeting was strained. Casey hated the way Randy was dressed. He was wearing jewelry that had been picked out for him by one of his girlfriends who had also dressed him. But in spite of it all, he did have class, and he was cute, and so charming. He kissed Casey on the cheek and there was something that made her know that he would call back. She wanted the children especially to have a solid foundation and constructive life, and she wanted happiness for herself too.

Casey would find that she would get tired easily. This had to do with the shock that she experienced as a result of the suicide. As good as she felt most of the time, she still had to deal with the shock. It was always there. Sometimes she felt like things were happening around her and she was observing what was going on, like being on the outside and looking in. It was an unbelievable that came and went, almost as if she had stepped out of her body and watched her life go on in front of her.

Then there was the feeling that things were just standing still. Casey learned to cope with these feelings so that she could cope. It took a while though, and eventually they went away. However, while she was having these periods that were attributed to the shock of the experience, this didn't mean that Casey couldn't function quite normally, because she was able to.

Casey totally was able to put Barry's death in its proper perspective after her automobile accident which occurred after she was married to Randy.

The shock of the accident seemed to work with the trauma that Casey was going through over the suicide and it had a positive effect on her. She was able to put the trauma of her life behind her. Could it have been the impact of the accident? It was like a good omen. Bizarre. Feelings of shock seemed to linger much longer than any other feelings that Casey had to deal with, especially guilt feelings which Casey seemed to be able to work out immediately.

Casey had a lot of challenges to overcome in her life and she had a lot to deal with. The most difficult challenge for Casey was that she had to be her own support team and she had to know her goals and where she was going.

16

Peggy had returned to New York and she was feeling a little depressed. She rushed to the analyst before going back to work to try to get it out.

It was depressing to her, returning. Leaving Casey made Peggy feel somewhat inadequate because she felt that she was Casey's support team and now Randy would be replacing that part of her life. This was hard for her. It was disappointing, it was self-inflicted. But it would work itself out in time.

Casey had fallen hook, line and sinker for Randy Edwards, and they were together all the time.

Everything was wonderful. Casey and Randy spent a lot of time with John and Lesley doing wonderful mundane family things that she had missed and they were together constantly. Even though Randy had been involved in another relationship, it was working out. He had no interest in seeing this other woman. Casey was divinely happy. She had never known what real happiness was really like. It felt great, and the children were great, and receptive to Randy, and doing quite well.

Casey and Randy loved the private moments that they had together, and the time they had with the children. It was almost like a fantasy. Along with their private moments, they were slowly starting to be seen at dinner, charity benefits, parties, the most important and best places in Chicago. They were the darlings of the social set, and traveling all over the world.

Casey's life was quite a bit different than most of her friends, but she handled the situation well. And of course, some of her friends changed. Peggy and she were very close and because they had been through so much and shared so much of their lives with each other, they were capable of dealing with stress situations and conflicts that occurred between them. Peggy was still carrying on her relationship with Charles Phillips and it did have its problems. One was Mary Ellen, Chuck's wife, who was Peggy's childhood friend and the daughter of her parents' best friends. It was an intense situation.

Mary Ellen had everything now that Charles was making big money. When he bought the Ritz Carleton, he was quoted in Forbes as the Man Of the Year, worth 800 million dollars. Peggy wanted him so badly that she thought of poisoning Mary Ellen at times. The most interesting thing about this whole relationship was that Peggy, through her friendship with Mary Ellen, knew that the reason Mary Ellen had been seeing a psychiatrist for the last 15 years was not because she couldn't cope with the children, and she was anything but helpless, but she really did not like having sex with her husband and, in fact, she really only cared about herself and her personal needs. She hated Chuck. She did like her three million dollar apartment on Park Avenue. All of her jewelry, furs, beautiful clothes and possessions, but she wanted independence and to be able to feel that she was her own person. This was something that Peggy and Casey could relate to because they had really been on their own. Mary Ellen had not. And in spite of the fact that Mary Ellen was establishing a solid career for herself, she would always be haunted by these feelings.

Peggy always was able to point out to Casey what not to do with Randy, but she could not follow her own advice. Casey tried to help Peggy because this was one area that she was an expert about, and when Peggy listened, it paid off.

Mary Ellen was calling Peggy a lot now and they were getting along great. It did make Chuck quite nervous, but Peggy had so much anger toward him at times that this was almost a form of revenge for her. Peggy was an evil person. She was beaten down in her life and always felt she was second to her sister and actually always felt that way in her life. This resentment to her parents made her vicious and mean. Although she tried to overcome these horrifying traits, she often had trouble with this and it made her psychotic and schizophrenic.

She hated Casey but she also loved her and admired her, and she loathed Mary Ellen because she wanted everything that Mary Ellen had. To know Peggy, one would think she was caring and even loving, but there was a mean, treacherous side to her and she could snap like that. She was relentless, jealous, controlling and domineering, overbearing, abusive, and self-centered, as well as very paranoid.

Mary Ellen told Peggy at lunch that she was mad for one of the decorators at her firm and that they had been going out for almost a year. They were not only together in the day time but in the evening too. And he was ten years younger than she was. When Mary Ellen told her that they hadn't gone to bed together yet, she couldn't believe it, but then again she knew Mary Ellen well and she had no reason to lie. Charles could accept the fact that his wife was frigid and that she was a good mother and beautiful, but this was a complete reversal and a real blow to his ego. Casey told Peggy that even though he said that it didn't bother him, it had to be eating him up inside.

Mary Ellen fucking another man besides Charles, was the funniest thing that crossed Casey's mind and every time she would think about it or talk to Peggy about it, she would roar. Charley would always call Casey when she was in New York, which made her feel a little uncomfortable due to his relationship with Peggy and her relationship with Peggy. This was something that Casey could not quite figure out and looking at this situation positively, it was cultivating a nice friendship with Charles and possibly keeping Peggy at the same time. She was always nice to Charles and Mary Ellen.

Casey and Mary Ellen were closer than they had been in a long time because they would see each other a lot through Margot, the three of whom were inseparable and best friends in the '60s. Through Mary Ellen is how Casey met Lauren.

Margot was dying of cancer, which was diagnosed shortly after her divorce, and all of these things had brought the three friends closer together. Margot had gone through a very stressful period with her divorce and now that she found out that the cancer from her mastectomy had spread, she had relinquished all of the independence that she had achieved, to become totally dependent on her family again. Her boyfriend dumped her, leaving her the husband who loved her to live with and see her through her dying days. This was overwhelming for Casey and Mary Ellen, but they were good friends and very supportive of Margot. Margot was a rebel and she was a good person.

Charley was very involved with Margot's life but he was much too egotistical to let it interfere with his own. He was tough and rough cut in spite of his accomplishments and lifestyle.

Casey really thought that Charley was inconsiderate and not really interested in Lauren's needs and rather than helping her in any way, he was using her, hurting her and she knew it and not really doing much for her. Even though she denied it, he was holding her back from other relationships and she was really not deriving anything from this one. He did not look at their relationship this way. To him it was just inflating his ego and sex.

17

Lauren was unhappy and concentrating her nervous energy into her job and getting some very successful results. Her relationship with Chuck was frustrating but she could only hope that it would change. Randy was with Casey all the time and they loved each others' company. It was like a fantasy, they did everything together. Casey was careful to slow things down even though Randy was more impulsive. It was getting so they spent all of their waking hours together and Casey, who had not even been to bed with him, would fantasize about the future. Randy was a challenge and could mean trouble, but she liked what she saw. He was careful not to be too aggressive; however, he was pretty fast moving. But because of the sensitivity of Casey's situation, being a widow for such a short time, and the emotional strain that she must have been going through, he was also careful and wanted her to feel perfectly comfortable with the progression of their relationship.

Everything was moving along beautifully. Casey was thinking to herself what it would be like to be in bed with Randy; the excitement that traveled through her body made all of her nerve endings tingle. It had been too long since she had really known what a real relationship was like and she had to take a chance because she wanted Randy Allen so much that she would not let herself be hurt.

Barry's breakdown had left more of an effect on Casey than she ever thought, even though she seemed to cope with the situation very well. There were some very deep-rooted feelings that would take her a long time to bring to the surface. Some of these things she could discuss with Randy and some were hard to talk about.

Everything was fantastic between Randy and Casey. He was very wealthy. Adorable, strong, tough, and a nice person. He made her feel wonderful and she did the same for him. They could laugh together and have fun, as well as be very serious and even work together. Casey fantasized about being married to him and about having him be John and Lesley's father, and she also had sexual fantasies about him.

Sleeping with Randy in their Mediterranean villa with the wind whistling and the smell of Rosemary and Myrtle in the air. Thurman, The Allen's driver and houseman was there to cook and always keep beer on ice for Randy, and champagne for Casey. He would drive them to Eden Roc and wait for them as well as chauffeur them to Monte Carlo, to parties and private dinners, it was ecstasy.

She wanted him very much but she was also afraid that he might just think that she was common if she jumped into bed with him. She wondered what he would think if he knew that she was spending her weekends fucking her brains out with friends and other suitors. Casey even accepted an occasional invitation to an orgy. This was before AIDS, this was the freedom of the '70s.

Randy was very delicate with Casey. He even taught her about sex and pleasure, and she was a great student. She went along with everything that he showed her and she loved it. Randy's ego exploded because there was so much gratification from all of these pleasures. It occasionally crossed his mind that Casey might have experienced some of these sexual pleasures, but it didn't even matter because she was so good and they enjoyed so much together. Casey knew that she was vulnerable and she was cautious. Randy wanted to be with Casey all the time and she felt the same about him. They traveled together and slowly started to appear in public at the best places. It was so exciting and they were so good together. The children loved Randy and he loved them. Casey could see his strength and she needed that.

Casey's picture was constantly in the paper taken at parties that she and Randy had attended, and the gossip columnists were constantly writing about them. Randy's wealth and power attracted the press and the David Alan Company was a nationally known company, receiving news coverage almost daily. Randy was the chairman of the board.

Casey loved the fact that gossip was not focusing on her wealth because she was sick of hearing that she was Sidney Rothschild's daughter, or worth millions. She just wanted to be herself and that's why the quiet moments that Randy and Casey had together were so important to both of them.

It took Casey a long time to be able to realize this but she did not miss Barry at all. And the less involved she had to be with his family, the happier she was. She did feel it was important to continue to see them and have a relationship with them because of the children, but they were so much beneath her that she felt she was lowering herself to be with them. But it was something that she had to do. They should have been thrilled that she chose to continue to have a relationship with them, but they didn't react like people of class and fine background. It was the right thing to do. They should have been most solicitous of her, but instead it was always the other way around, and it especially hurt Casey because her dad was the only nice person to Barry when he was ill.

Barry had had a bad relationship with his father and mother. Ethel hardly ever went to see him in the hospital. It was always Sidney who gave him confidence and made him feel good about himself, and Barry even made $100,000 as a fiduciary of Sidney's estate.

Max and Ethel hardly did a thing to help Casey with the children. After Barry died, they were not even very supportive, but Casey wanted the children to have a grandparent image and always taught them to show love and respect to their grandparents, which could become more difficult if they weren't returning their feelings.

Randy gave Casey all of the support that she needed and wasn't getting from others. Randy made her strong and able to cope. Casey needed to cope now and she knew this. This relationship was like a fantasy. Randy being the chairman of the board of his company could travel when he wanted, and work as long or short of a day as he wanted. He was able to sleep until noon if he wished, or be up at sunrise. Casey knew that this was what she wanted, and she loved the flexibility that Randy had to be able to do what he wanted to do. Randy was very much a part of Casey's life and family, even though she had not met Randy's children yet, but they were living out of town or away at school and this wasn't as easy for him.

She would be holding hands with Peter and running through a beautiful rose garden in the country with just some flimsy chiffon material thrown around her. Peter would inadvertently be pursuing Casey through his touches and a certain glance that would catch her eye. She was dressed very ethereally with a crown of daisies on her head and her nipples were erect showing through the flimsy material covered her body. And as they ran through the garden into the woods, the dream would end. Another dream that Casey would have was that Peter absconded with her at her wedding and the two of them disappeared. Again she appeared in this dream barely clothed. It was very erotic.

Casey's life with Peter went from fantasy to reality. They both wanted each other so much but Casey knew this was wrong for her. She did have problems at times because she loved to play with him, which was totally unrealistic. She could go weeks and months without actually being with him but they were both tormented by this. Casey was in New York with Randy and on her way to Bloomingdale's, walking around the corner of Madison and 61st Street, and she ran directly into Peter. It was unbelievable, not planned, and a very sexually exciting experience. The shock was exhilarating and Casey's sexual suppressions were surfacing. She kissed Peter and told him how nice it was to see him, but she left him immediately, knowing that this could threaten her relationship with Randy, which was the last thing that she wanted to do. She loved Randy, he was always the one.

Casey was at the top. With Randy she enhanced his image and he enhanced hers. They complemented each other beautifully. Gossip columnists were writing about them. They were always mentioned wherever they had been seen around town, and every time they entered a party, all eyes were on them. Casey felt vulnerable and felt like people were talking about her, but Randy had no problem with what people were saying. They both thrived on it. Casey wanted to marry Randy and she didn't want to see Peter. She didn't want to know Peter, but he was always there. Randy loved Casey but he wasn't as anxious to marry again as she was. This wasn't going to stop Casey. She was either going to be Randy's wife or she would go on to try to make a life for herself. Casey knew she had everything going for herself and she was going to make a life for Leslye and John. Casey was very strong and of able character and she knew that being beautiful was a shortcoming that she had to beware of and always be on guard.

It was almost immediately after Barry's death when Casey realized that she had to show her strength because Barry's parents had immediately started to take advantage of her financially, and if she wasn't smart enough to catch it, it could have happened repeatedly. The things that they did were reprehensible. They took certain privileges away from her that she should have been allowed to have from the company that were provided for Barry. The first circumstance was not being able to charge telephone calls to the company. Casey's attorney took over with that and many more small incidents. Casey was just relieved that she could be independent and that she didn't need these people. They were cruel, angry, heartless and insensitive.

While all of these adjustments and problems were going on, it was fortunate that Casey looked forward to being with Randy. She loved the time she spent with him. She always wanted to be with him. They also spent a lot of time with the kids. This was the best. Sometimes it takes a person a long time to really realize how wonderful first priorities, family and children are. Sometimes it takes a terrible tragedy, but when Casey could say herself how wonderful this was and she really knew that this was what life was all about, this was a great feeling. It made her feel real peace of mind.

It was during Barry's illness that she knew she only wanted what was best for the children and she knew she wanted a real strong family unit. Casey, being a wealthy only child, was not a self-destructive person, and she knew how to take care of herself. Randy was big time, and she was going to make sure that she got him.

18

The time had come in their relationship where Casey could see that it was more beneficial for herself than for Randy.

It was making her feel less comfortable and nervous and she was becoming stagnant because she could see that she had reached a point in her life where she was going nowhere. She now wanted to be married to Randy and with some fear she told him of her feelings, and what was disturbing her. They had reached a point in their relationship where she was going to have to put their love on the line. Marriage was the only direction that she could see her relationship with Randy going.

He was so powerful, and she did not want to get lost in his identity.

Barry had sane enough moments that Casey and he could communicate, and he was able to tell her what was going on with the computers and how patients were removing money from bank accounts through credit cards for very large sums.

Casey thought this would be a last hope for Barry, even better than the rock group, if he could break the scam and devulge what was going on in the hospital on his very same floor, practically in front of him. She really thought this might snap him out of his depression and help him. They worked on uncovering this scheme together. It was very exciting and brought them closer together. The turmoil and freedom of the seventies had an effect on their lives, and as Casey would continue to grow and mature and find out how brilliant she really was, she would see that this evolution would be recurring in the nineties. It is true that everything does go in cycles.

She told Randy about the scheme after they were married and he was very interested because he was feeling stagnant and felt that this would be a youthful resurgence for him. Casey was flourishing and glowing. Her life was growing and she was becoming smarter and more clever than Randy. Her ideas for running the business were better and he was feeling threatened by her. He had been the force behind her motivation and she was growing and developing, and Randy was starting to feel inferior with a poor self-image. He knew deep down in his heart that the spark that he lit for Casey throughout their relationship and their marriage was out. He was upset and devastated, but could not and would not deal with it, so he took out his aggressions in other ways. His bad characteristics always remained, however, they were more apparent when he was having problems. He had some heavy psychological problems and would not face them. He had a reputation of lying and cheating that Casey tried to cover up and help save face but she was tired of giving more than she was getting. Casey helped him through one trauma in his life, but he was older now and people were less tolerant, and didn't care about him. He was losing his power and had dropped out of the main stream. He certainly didn't intimidate. Without his power he was nothing and Casey was everything.

Casey could see that she needed to depend less and less on Randy's expertise, and that she was much sharper than he was of mind and body. Randy was falling and certainly from the limelight that Casey was able to put him in, the worst scenario that is yet to come in order to end this story of lust` love hate passion, deceitful revenge and corruption, there is a change of identity involving a serial killer who casey suspects could be her husband and not only that, she thinks he went to John Grossman and had a complete face and body change. Plastic surgery changed him completely, it made him look totally different, Randy was experiencing a surge of sexual excitement that stimulated his sick sense to kill because nobody knew who this killer really was. Casey knew, and she didn't want to believe it, however the facts were there and pointing to Randy.

He had gone off the deep end. Casey felt that the children's and her life were in danger, She was dealing with a psychotic who had really fucked up and would stop at nothing to get his revenge. He was terribly afraid of rejection and this had Casey most concerned because she could not go to the police, and he wanted to marry her with someonelse's idenity and torture her for revenge. He had plastic surgery, was another person with a new idenity, but this was Randy. He was milking her of all of her assets, through a huge insurance policy and putting huge amounts of money in Caymen Island bank accounts. Casey had to end this at once, for her own safety. She told John about this lunatic, and they needed to be protected. Barry who was really ill, and he couldn't be blamed for his actions or helped. He was a tortured soul and his horrible fate was not to be questioned because he was so ill there was no logical explanation for it. Randy was just evil and sicker than anyone had ever imagined. Ari, the real man in Casey's life tried to protect her and help her. He was sure that this serial killer was Randy and that he had to be stopped. There was too much evidence pointing to him, he had disappeared and all of these peculiar and coincidental things that were happening to Casey and the children seemed to point to Randy. He had flipped out. Who was this psycho This was worse than an alien invasion and the only way that Casey could continue her life in peace was to stop it and perscribe a healthy diet to successfully go on. Perhaps a diet of sex and vegetables or perhaps she has had enough of that and the only solution was to eradicate Randy. The question was how without hurting too many who were involved, especially all of the children.

Her friend and politically connected, a very powerful person could be a way to combat this whole devastation, and this was what Casey with the help of Ari had to do in order to have a good life and some stability for the children and herself.

They started by erecting a plan and this would end all the Turmoil and stress that was going on. Casey's goal was to get it done and get off of this rollercoaster and be able to get on with her life.

There was a certain sadness, because everything she had, and loved had been upset because of a jealous moment in her life, which she knew she was to blame. All had to be changed and very carefully so she could get on with her life.

(closing dialogue)

Randy was caught in the middle of committing a crime And after his confession he was put away for life to 125years. Fate has played a funny role in Casey's life, she has been involved with many promenient and powerful people, both men and women. A lot of her experiences had to do with being in the right place at the right time. ☺wink.

19

THE END...........

Dialogue: What has happened to you my darling, we had it all and you are my very dearest love, life cannot be the same without you, we are so great together. I am here for you, and will do anything to help you. You know you can count on me

For anything. I will not have you be a prisnor, you mean too much to me, we are so wonderful together and everything that we do is with such love and compassion for each other that is more than most people experience in a lifetime together. I hope I don't loose you, life can be evil but you don't deserve this, you have the wrong woman behind you and she will ruin you and you will end up a broken man. This is a sadness, you are too smart and have done so much to help not only yourself succeed but to help so many other's. I know there is a way out and I will find the best treatment for you, and you will find your independence again, I will make you that promise. Stay with me, I don't want to lose you, I feel like I am watching you from a ship this is so unbelievable and I don't want to lose you, my husband, I will do anything to help you.

Life has many strange twists and turns and I will do anything to help you, you don't deserve this sentence and I will work around this to help you my beautiful, smart, passionate friend.

We will succeed, we always do. There is a future and you deserve it for both of us.

Where are you my love? Please come back. We are so great together. Randy was getting weaker with age and he suffered from Parkensses disease and it was very complicated.

20

This is a very complicated twist to the whole story of Casey, because as always in her life there were many twists and turns and now she is involved in more than a novel situation, which we all hope will not turn into a survival situation or a financial struggle, this is just the beginning of the end of this very passionate novel. Casey knows that her passionate lover will in still some good to take care of her and that she with her kindness and truthfulness will take care of her, and she, Lesyle and John and their families will all take care and be alright.

The world in it's grave situation cannot deal with terriorism or get the United States Of America back to being the strongest country with the way that the left and right have changed, the next president will have to pull it together and at least with the help of congress and the senate not let it become a quagmire and start to move this country forward with peace and solidarity and then address this nation's economy. Life is not a perfect situation, and will have problems that will need to be solved always. If you look at life when it was far less simple than it is now there were always problems, fighting, and her challenge would be to keep her life centered, and love with all her heart too the moon and back her children, and grandchildren and all of her extended family, and continue to live to it's fullest and always be there for the ones she loves!

This novel could depict anyone from the lowest point on earth to the height of society.